Flipping the Switch

Flipping the Switch

Katherine Covell

Somewhat Grumpy Press Inc.

ISBN
978-1-7776898-1-0 (paperback)
978-1-7776898-2-7 (eBook)

First Printing, 2021
Second Printing, 2021

CONTENTS

ACKNOWLEDGEMENT ix

DEDICATION x

Prologue | Rebecca, November 2018 1

PART 1: BEFORE 1980-2018

1 | Alison and Simon 6

2 | Alison and Simon 13

3 | Ian and Fiona 18

4 | Alison and Simon 24

5 | Alison and Simon 30

6 | Nigel 35

7 | Ian and Fiona 42

8 | Justin 48

9 | Justin 56

CONTENTS

10 | Ian and Fiona 61

11 | Alison and Simon 67

12 | Justin 72

13 | Ian and Fiona 77

14 | Nigel 82

15 | Justin 87

PART 2: THAILAND January-March 2018

16 | The Meet and Greet 92

17 | Getting to Know Malcolm 98

18 | Good Times 103

19 | Nigel Tells his Story 109

20 | Introducing Criss-Cross 115

21 | Just Joking 120

22 | Saved by the Sting 126

23 | The Trolley Problem 131

24 | Thou Shalt Not Kill 136

25 | Malevolent or Benevolent? 141

26 | Justin's Break 146

27 | Death and Persuasion 151

28 | Nigel Returns Home 156

29 | Ian and Fiona Leave 161

30 | Alison's Plans 167

31 | Justin's Retreat 172

PART 3: AFTER April-September 2018

32 | Justin 178

33 | Ian and Fiona 184

34 | Nigel and Malcolm 189

35 | Alison and Simon 196

36 | Ian and Fiona 202

37 | Nigel and Malcolm 207

CONTENTS

38 | Alison and Simon **213**

39 | Ian and Fiona **218**

40 | The MOE Gang **224**

Epilogue | Rebecca, March 2019-November 2020 **230**

AUTHOR'S NOTE **237**
ABOUT THE AUTHOR **238**

If anyone enjoys reading this story, it's because of the outstanding editing job by my favourite editor Tim, who also happens to be my son, and the excellent advice given by my most useful critic, adviser, and brilliant partner Brian. Most inspirational have been the wonderful staff at the Hilton Arcadia Resort in Phuket. A special thank you to Nutch, Petch, and Eva—you have given me so many wonderful memories.

For Bill and the rest of *my* MOE gang who inspired this story, although they are nothing like these characters.

Rebecca, November 2018

The rain had been drumming endlessly on the windows of Inspector Rebecca Youngman's office, and now the sky was darkening. Yawning and rubbing her eyes, she looked at the pile of documents still needing her attention before she could leave for the day. Of all the cases she had worked on, this one was the most baffling. The press called it the Met Murder. Rebecca thought of it as the horrible heiress homicide. There were so many who had good reason to wish the rich bitch dead. She had been involved in at least three traffic fatalities, and she had a well-earned reputation for seducing married men and then letting their wives know. The most obvious suspects, Rebecca thought, were a couple of university professors. Samantha had killed their daughter, on their daughter's twenty-first birthday, in a horrendous example of dangerous driving. But it turned out the professors were in England at the time. In fact, no matter how hard Rebecca looked, each suspect had an alibi that had proven airtight. This case had been one frustration after another.

She had spent more time trying to solve this case than any other. After months of chasing leads, investigating potential suspects, and interviewing persons of interest and potential witnesses, Rebecca had nothing. Her final report was due today. She had come in early to review all the information and had not taken a break. But, she realized, there was no way she could get through the pile of documents still in front of her. Sighing, she picked up the folder on the top of the pile. It contained the contemporaneous details of the scene. Maybe, just maybe, she thought, there would be something there that she had missed. She read it through one last time.

It had been a cool, but sunny, Saturday afternoon in May. As usual after a matinee at the Met opera, Lincoln Square was teeming with the almost four thousand attendees who were leaving at about the same time. Many were standing around in small groups chatting. It was a diverse group. There were many elderly patrons. Walkers and wheelchairs were plentiful. There were young people casually dressed in jeans and running shoes. And there were the middle-aged in traditional opera-going garb of gowns and tuxes. Among the crowd was the notorious Samantha Costner. With her height, bright red hair, loud voice, excessive jewellery, and striped faux fur jacket she would have stood out. But when a shot rang out and she lay bleeding, no one, it seemed, had noticed her, or seen a thing. Not even her boy-toy date could provide any useful information about what happened.

Thousands of hours of subsequent interviews had provided no information. Most likely no one wanted to get involved with the Costner family, Rebecca supposed. Or maybe all the dramatic diva deaths in opera had inured the fans to the real thing, she thought. The opera had been Puccini's *Tosca*, one Rebecca had enjoyed when she'd seen it some years ago.

The opera lovers, perhaps thinking it was an extension of a typical opera plot, were reported to have just stepped over her body, avoiding the blood that was seeping from it. No one touched her jewels or her purse. Presumably, the opera attendees were focused on getting a cab while one was still available. There were never enough at the end of a performance.

The perp among them, Rebecca thought to herself, yawning. He, or she, had simply blended with the crowd and got away. She scanned the report one last time, hit submit, and put the files into a box for transfer to the archives. She accepted that this would have to remain an unsolved case, at least for now. A few months ago, she'd registered to attend a cold case conference next spring. Perhaps there, she'd get a fresh perspective on the case and make some progress. It seemed inconceivable that Samantha's murderer would never be found.

Thinking about the conference, she felt better. At the very least, it would allow her to get away for a while. It had been a long time since Rebecca had experienced international travel. It had been even longer since she had enjoyed a vacation. At least the conference was something to look forward to, she consoled herself, as she put her coat on and picked up her umbrella. In the meantime, she had only half an hour to get home to baby Leah before the sitter had to leave. It would be a brisk and very wet walk to her apartment.

PART 1: BEFORE
1980-2018

1

Alison and Simon

Alison was exhausted. She had started at six that morning, serving the breakfast crowd at Dan's Café. It had not gone well. Her second customer was a middle-aged business type of guy who asked for avocado toast. As patiently as she could, she reviewed the menu with him, noting that there was no such option. He remained steadfast, and loud.

"I want avocado toast!" He whined as petulantly as a two-year-old asking for candy. "You have avocados doncha? You have toast doncha? So, bring me some avocado toast. What's wrong with you people in Maine?" Heads turned. Some customers looked shocked, and some were laughing.

Alison flushed in embarrassment. She muttered to him and went to ask the chef if he could make some damn avocado toast for the jerk at table five. Having heard the exchange and feeling sorry for Alison, he agreed.

"Must be from Manhattan," the chef said, "I hear it's becoming very trendy there."

"Yea, well this is Bangor." Alison responded flipping her blond ponytail, her hazel eyes glinting with anger.

The jerk didn't leave her a tip, and spoiled Alison's mood for the rest of her shift. Finishing at eleven that morning, Alison had enough time to rush home, shower, and change before a four-hour afternoon stint as a clerk at the local bodega. This can't go on, Alison said to herself.

A few months earlier, she had walked away from a bad marriage, taking her children, four-year-old Michael and two-year-old Melody, with her. Leaving had not been easy. Marrying at seventeen and having two children before she was twenty-two, Alison had no chance to finish school or prepare for a meaningful career. Being acutely aware of this, and with the children to care for, Alison had not wanted to leave the marriage. But she could no longer cope with a husband who routinely had sex with other women, and who, on more than one occasion, had commented that she was a less exciting sexual partner than one of his hook-ups. He had even taken a Playboy centrefold to bed one night and then told Alison how her body compared to the nude model. Alison's, of course, was not as good. Who did he think he was, she had wondered? He was no Adonis. She left within a month of that incident. Life was difficult, but she at least had regained her dignity and sense of self-worth.

The divorce, unlike the marriage, was painless. She had been receiving some child support from the children's father, but it was not nearly enough for rent and food, let alone all the other expenses. And now that he had emigrated to Australia, Alison supposed it was only a matter of time before he stopped paying child support. Alison wanted to be independent. She knew she had to earn a degree to get a decent job. She figured that if she could get subsidized care for the children, and if she studied part-time, she just might be able to improve her situation. The money she earned at the bodega, together with her child support and a student loan, just might make education possible. The avocado toast guy was the impetus she needed to make it happen. That next day, she gave her notice for Dan's, and visited the library to find out about applying to university.

* * *

A month later, she was on her way to her first class at the local college, an evening psychology lecture. It had been a busy but satisfying month. The campus, she thought, was the perfect place to start her new life. It had a daycare for the children of students, staff, and faculty, which seemed perfect for Michael and Melody. It had a subsidized cafeteria where she could buy nutritious meals at reasonable prices, and better yet, she got a job there working five hours a day. It paid more than working at the bodega and didn't require travelling time. Her sense that everything was going to work out well was reinforced when she noted an ad on the student housing board that looked perfect for her. It was a small basement apartment in a house near the college. The rent was low in exchange for helping the owner with shopping and yard work. She went right there and met the landlady and owner of the house, Mrs. Elizabeth Burke.

Alison worried that the children may not be welcome. But as a recent and lonely widow with no family, Mrs. Burke was thrilled to have Alison and her children in the house. It didn't take long before they all got along so well that Mrs. Burke decided she would be a surrogate grandma to Melody and

Michael, and a surrogate mother to Alison. Alison's mother had died years before, and she didn't know anything about her father. Mrs. Burke offered to take care of the children in the evenings when Alison had evening classes. The children delighted in the attention.

To ease into her new lifestyle, Alison started with two courses, Introduction to Psychology and Contemporary English Literature. She wasn't sure that these choices would help her get a job, but she wanted to start with subjects she was interested in.

Feeling apprehensive on her first day, Alison arrived at her psychology class early. There were already several students in the lecture hall. She chose a seat near the front. Among the other students drifting in, one caught her attention. His long and windblown dark curly hair, scruffy beard, and his loose jeans and baggy sweatshirt gave him a dishevelled look that Alison found very appealing. He was clutching an old leather satchel with books spilling out of it. Looking as awkward as Alison felt, he scanned the room and appeared to notice her looking at him. He grinned. She looked away embarrassed. He looks closer to my age than most the students here, Alison thought, and like someone who'd be a good friend. There's nothing like a divorce and a move to lose friends, she mused. The professor entered the room, and the chatter died down. After a short introductory lecture, the professor spread sheets of paper on the table. Each had the names of six students who would form a discussion group. Discussion groups would meet each week after the lecture.

"Hi, I'm Simon Leeland," said the dishevelled guy, as he

joined the group to which Alison had been assigned. She was delighted that this peer and possible friend was in her group. The other students in their group were younger. Two did not return after the first week. Some weeks later, a third, Mary Monaghan, left to attend the Joffrey Ballet School in New York City and follow her dream of becoming a ballerina. Aside from Alison and Simon, that left only Brianna Miles, a shy girl who kept to herself. Although Alison missed the friendly and cheerful Mary, she enjoyed having more time with Simon. Alison learned that, like her, Simon had been away from education for many years. He had worked a variety of jobs including driving an airport taxi and working as a first aid attendant. Alison felt comfortable with him.

* * *

Five weeks into the course, Alison noticed a poster advertising a Julian Bream concert. There was no time to check the details since she was on her way to class, but she was eager to go. She loved classical guitar and was surprised that someone of Bream's stature would be playing in Bangor. She decided to ask Simon if he'd like to go with her, as long as the concert was a night Mrs. Burke could take care of the children.

Simon, although somewhat taken aback and amused by her question, happily accepted her invitation. Before the next class, Alison went back to the power pole on which the Bream concert poster had been tacked. After checking the place and time she didn't know whether to laugh or cry. The notice was over a year old. The concert was long past. Alison was mortified.

"You really didn't need to go to such lengths to ask me out," Simon said, when a red-faced Alison explained her error. "Why don't I take you for a beer after class tonight instead?" A greatly relieved Alison agreed. She called Mrs. Burke to let her know she'd be back later than usual.

Relaxing at the pub, Simon and Alison laughed over the error. They discovered they shared many interests in addition to classical guitar. It was the best evening Alison could remember for many years. She was thrilled when Simon asked if he could meet the children and if they could all go out together.

The following week, Simon picked up Alison and the children, and they went for a walk and ice cream. A few weeks and more family outings later, Alison decided that asking Simon to a non-existent concert was the best mistake of her life.

Although Alison was, at first, reluctant to think of Simon as anything more than a friend, his easy manner and his obvious pleasure at spending time with Michael and Melody wore down her defences. Simon spent more and more time at Alison's apartment over the next few months, and over the Christmas break. He met Mrs. Burke, and she told Alison he seemed a good man. Mrs. Burke invited Simon, Alison, and the children to have Christmas dinner with her.

"I feel like I am in a Hallmark movie," Mrs. Burke commented as they sat around the table which was laden with roast turkey and all the trimmings. "This is so wonderful."

Two weeks later, Alison and Simon were enjoying coffee at the kitchen table and chatting about the upcoming semester.

Michael ran up to Simon and said, "Why don't you just move in with us, you're always here anyway?"

"Great idea," Simon said with a grin. "Would that be okay? We could share the cost of rent and we could be together while we study. And there's lots of studying. Maybe we'll go on and get PhDs? I can cook, and I love being with Michael and Melody—well and you of course, I love you all."

"I'm not so sure about the PhDs," Alison responded, grinning.

"Yea!" Michael was jumping up and down. "We can be a real family again with Grandma Burke and a dad."

2

Alison and Simon

"I can't believe that we're both going for PhDs. You'd think the financial struggles and exhausting lifestyle would have turned us away from more university."

"True," replied Simon. "But as much as things have been difficult, it's also been great. All those discussions we had in class like capitalism versus communism, democracy compared to authoritarianism, even about Freud's concept of penis envy and feminism. I loved all that. Remember how we used to spend so much of our time at the library and the archives. And remember how proud the kids were when you received your honours BSc? Michael shouting 'Yea Mom!' from the bleachers, and Melody running up on stage to give you a hug. Imagine how they're gonna feel when you are Dr. Mom."

For their graduate studies, Simon had decided he wanted to specialize in history. Alison wanted to continue with psychology. The first hurdle was to find universities that were suitable and accepted them both since they did not want to live apart for the next six years or more. After a few tense months waiting to hear the results of their applications, not only were they both accepted by the same university in New York, but it also offered each of them a scholarship and teaching assistantship. That made the move attractive and financially feasible. The university also offered low-rent family housing to graduate students. It all seemed too good to be true. It was. Although the early years together had been a struggle of insufficient finances and time, they seemed easy compared with those spent in graduate school.

The first challenge was moving from Maine and Grandma Burke. The move was particularly difficult for Michael, now ten years old. As well as having to leave the only grandmother he had ever known, he was upset about leaving his friends, his school, the beaches he loved to play on, and his baseball team. Melody, who had a much easier temperament than Michael, happily adapted to her new grade three classroom. Moving into student housing turned out to be a much greater challenge.

Living in student housing had advantages. Costs were low. There were lots of other young families in their building, and there was a "free store" where students left clothes, toys, and furniture that their children had outgrown, for other students to take as needed. But there were many disadvantages. The apartments were small and the walls thin. It was not unusual for sleep or study to be disrupted by crying children or arguing parents. Worse were the cockroaches.

The first night Alison and Simon slept there, they heard an unfamiliar ticking sound after they turned all the lights out. When it persisted, Simon got up and went into the living room to see what was causing the sound. As soon as he turned on the light, he knew. It was a scene Hitchcock might have directed. What seemed like hundreds of cockroaches were scurrying from all parts of the room into the baseboards around its perimeter. The next morning, Simon bought a bed from a family who were moving out. No more sleeping on or near the floor. They found beds at a local thrift store for Michael and Melody. Alison bought nightlights for every plug in the apartment.

* * *

The first two years of graduate school went by in a frenzied blur of activity. Both Simon and Alison had mandatory classes with many additional hours of reading and essay writing as well as their teaching assistantships. Simon also worked fifteen hours a week as a private tutor to help with finances. It was challenging to find time to spend with the children, let alone to shop, clean, and cook healthy meals. Michael responded to the chaos and lack of attention by skipping school.

Alison never forgot the day they got the letter from the department of education telling them they could apply to have the druid religion recognized but, until it was, a druid holiday was not acceptable for absence. Michael's self-written excuse notes were extraordinarily creative.

By year three, they had completed their required courses, and Alison and Simon spent more time at home with the children. They limited studying to when the children were in school, and after the children were in bed. A family outing became the highlight of each weekend. They enjoyed going to the Bronx Zoo, the Natural History Museum, and Central Park. A highlight was going to see *Swan Lake* at Christmas.

They were delighted to find that Mary Monaghan was dancing the lead role. Alison and Simon introduced her to the children after the performance and they exchanged fond memories of those first few weeks at college in Maine. Over time, family life became more normal. Michael settled down, made good friends, and soon excelled at school. Melody continued to be her ever-sunny self, loving everyone and everything.

The focus for Simon and Alison now was thesis research. Simon chose the question of whether Hitler was inspired by the Armenian genocide. Simon's choice was motivated in part by his Armenian heritage, and in part by his pacifism. It had bothered him for some time that Hitler had referred to the genocide in ways that suggested he saw it as a model for the Nazi programs of extermination. Was Hitler's final solution inspired by the 1915 massacre of over one million Armenians, as some historians as argued? Hitler had asked "who speaks today of the extermination of the Armenians." Did this statement reflect a belief in the impunity of those who commit genocide? Did the massacre of the Armenians provide Hitler a model for extermination? Historians did not agree on these questions. Simon wanted to find the answer.

Alison wanted to study how children grew into adults who behaved violently to others. Three cases she had learned about as an undergraduate student particularly puzzled her. One was a fifteen-year-old high school student who had murdered his entire family: his parents, his younger brother, and his younger sister. It was a particularly memorable case because he was found not guilty by reason of insanity, committed to a state mental hospital, and escaped soon after, never to be found. Another case was a seventeen-year, John Catermain, who stabbed to death his mother and father while the family was on a camping trip. He claimed his parents had been abusive. Then there was Eleanor Tator, who was only ten years old when she was found guilty in the strangling death of a toddler. The media reported that she killed for the fun of it, but in court it came out that she had been abused. None of this made sense to Alison. Murder was not normally a symptom of mental illness, and surely abuse could be reported and dealt with. And why would anyone think that a little girl would kill for fun? Alison wanted to examine the backgrounds of children who had been convicted of killing their parents. Maybe later, she thought, she would research adults who kill children.

3

Ian and Fiona

As a teenager, Ian MacLean knew one thing for sure. He did not want to become a coal miner like his grandfather, his dad, or his uncles. Growing up in Glace Bay, Nova Scotia, Ian was all too familiar with the dangers of mining. He also recognized that the declining value of coal was leading to the deterioration of his community. He would, he determined, follow the advice given in folk musician Stan Rogers' song, and go "Down the Road." To do that, he learned in discussions with his priest, he needed to get good grades in high school, and then at the University College of Cape Breton. He never regretted taking Father O'Leary's advice.

In his first year at the college, Ian took courses in Celtic Music, English, Sociology, and Religious Studies. To his surprise, he enjoyed his classes in comparative religions the most. He was interested in the diversity of religious traditions, and the link between cults and religious movements. Much of what he learned seemed inconsistent with what he had learned about the church from his years of Sunday school, and later his involvement with the local church youth club. He wanted to learn more. And so, at the end of his two years at the college, he moved to Halifax where he enrolled in Dalhousie University. Living in student housing and majoring in religious studies, Ian was content, with one exception. He was lonely.

Spending Saturday nights alone at the student pub was a novel experience that Ian enjoyed when he first went to Halifax. After living in a town where everyone knew you and everything you did, anonymity was a delightful reprieve. But the novelty wore off and he longed for friendship—preferably female, with benefits, he thought to himself. He investigated options for student activity that would allow him to meet students other than those few who were in his classes. The female students he had met in his classes either seemed too old, or too boring, and none had shown any interest in him. Who would, he sometimes wondered, looking in the mirror at his lanky frame, ginger hair, and light blue eyes.

He joined the Student Life Committee. Its mandate was to work on ensuring accessible, diverse, and inclusive events for students, and develop policy regarding student life. Ian thought these were laudable goals. Joining the Committee turned out to be a life changing decision. It was there he met and fell in love with Fiona Macintyre, a petite woman with short curly black hair and sparkling green eyes.

Like Ian, Fiona had grown up in Cape Breton. But her life had differed greatly from Ian's. Whereas Ian had one older and three younger siblings, Fiona was an only child. While Ian had lived in a small company house in a declining neighbourhood and town, Fiona had lived in a large home on the shores of the beautiful Bras D'Or Lake in the scenic village of Baddeck. But they shared a love of Celtic music, nature, children, and a desire to help those in need: Ian through some form of religious activity or church, and Fiona through social work. They also shared a powerful attraction to each other, and, soon after they met, a passionate sexual relationship. Within a month of meeting, they were inseparable. Within six months, they were engaged and had planned out their future. They would, they decided, live, work, and raise a family in Halifax.

* * *

Not long after graduation, Ian became the minister for a local non-denominational church, a community-oriented institution he believed in. It was a perfect fit. Ian inherited a lively and diverse congregation who welcomed him and Fiona into their community. A month later, Fiona started work as a child protection worker. Fiona was excited about working with families instead of just reading about them, and she enjoyed her role as the minister's wife. With help from their parents, they were able to purchase an older home within walking distance of the church. The house was close to schools and parks, and it had a garden large enough to grow vegetables. Their dreams were coming true. After a year of settling into their new lives, the MacLean's decided it was time to start their family.

When they were dating, Ian and Fiona had shared their wishes for children. Fiona wanted two or three; Ian, who had grown up with four siblings, wanted at least four. They planned to have three, and then assess whether a fourth was desirable. But when the time came to consider a pregnancy, Fiona realized that although she wanted to raise children, giving birth was no longer important to her. Her education and her daily experiences had changed her.

Fiona had known of children who were neglected or abused in Baddeck. But she did not know how pervasive the maltreatment of children appeared to be. In her university courses, Fiona had been shocked to learn of the numbers of abused and neglected children, at the amount of red tape that was involved in removing a child from an abusive or neglectful home, and how difficult it was to find appropriate foster families for those who were removed. She learned of cases where child welfare agencies sent children to live in motel rooms because there were no families to care for them. And she learned of many children left with or returned to abusive parents only to die.

Some cases she learned about continued to haunt her. She could not forget her professor telling the class about the infant who died of dehydration and neglect in her crib despite repeated reports to child protection and medical authorities; another whose mother watered down her formula while assuring social workers she was fine; and a toddler sent to live with her aunt and uncle, despite their history of abuse, and beaten to death. Fiona was grateful that she had not experienced such horrendous situations since she started working with child protection, but she had become acutely aware of the numbers of children who desperately needed good foster or adoptive, families. The lack of placement options was an almost daily problem for the agency since there were so many children in dire circumstances. Fiona worried incessantly about the children in her case load who needed temporary out of home care. What could she do? How could she help? As she thought about these children, she became convinced that she and Ian should care for as many children as possible without having any themselves. She decided that they would become foster and adoptive parents, and that they would always give priority to the children most in need of care. She felt an enormous sense of relief having made this decision. But what about Ian. How would he feel? How could she convince him? Fiona was nervous. Ian had often talked about how much he wanted to be a dad and how exciting it would be when they were pregnant. She felt terrible about having to renege on their agreement and upset Ian, but she knew she had to.

* * *

One midsummer evening, when it wasn't raining for once, Fiona suggested a walk in Point Pleasant Park. It was a place where they both always felt relaxed. They stopped at Black Rock Beach and sat at a picnic table to enjoy the view of the ocean. Fiona could not relax. Taking a deep breath, and putting her shaking hands in her coat pockets, she told Ian how she felt.

He sat, staring at her, saying nothing. Her anxiety mounting, Fiona stood up and walked a few steps away. She then stopped and turned to face him. Ian was standing with a broad smile on his face. "Nothing would make me happier. I have been thinking the same thing but didn't say anything because I thought you wanted the pregnancies." He opened his arms; she fell into them. "As you know, my love, it will not be easy. A lot of these kids have had it rough, and they'll be difficult. But what could be better than us caring for these children. No matter how difficult they are, we'll take care of them as God would want us to do."

4

Alison and Simon

PhDs in hand, Alison and Simon had expected life to become more relaxing. Reality set in when they each started positions as assistant professors and moved out of student housing. They were lucky to find an apartment that allowed the children, now in grades eleven and twelve, to stay in their schools. They were even luckier to be hired as professors by the same university. But the demands of family, students, and the publish or perish ethos of the university meant constant exhaustion. University bureaucracy was frustrating, and preparing grades had an unexpected element of risk.

Although the widespread student protests of the Vietnam War were long finished, Alison was always aware of the potential for violence on campus. There were few campus shootings, but as a professor she learned she was a potential target for students annoyed with their grades. She recalled hearing about a math professor in California who was shot and killed by a student who had failed an exam, and a Latin professor in Florida who was shot and wounded by a student unhappy with their course mark.

"What are you supposed to do with students who get lousy grades or fail?" Alison asked Simon one day. "These incidents I am hearing about make me think you have to give everyone a pass to avoid being shot. It's insane."

While Simon and Alison were struggling with the demands of academia, Michael and Melody were doing well. With his classic good looks, blond cowlick bangs, and natural intelligence, Michael was popular with his peers and his teachers. Once he settled down, Michael excelled at school. His grades in English and History were stellar. The rest were average or above. He became a valued member of the school debating team and thoroughly enjoyed the inter-school and inter-state debating competitions, especially when there was overnight travel involved. By grade twelve, Michael decided he wanted to study law and international relations. He thought that would allow him a career either as a diplomat, a foreign policy consultant, or a human rights lawyer. He wasn't sure which would be more interesting, but he knew each would allow travel and lots of opportunities to meet interesting, if not influential, people. Just as his parents finished their university education, Michael was planning his.

Melody was less interested in academics than her brother. Her art teacher, Miss Frances Fowler, inspired her interests and career direction. One art class, Miss Fowler had told Melody's class the story of the so-called cellist of Sarajevo. Vedran Smajlović had been the principal cellist of the Sarajevo Opera. He also played in the Sarajevo Philharmonic Orchestra, the Symphony Orchestra RTV Sarajevo, and the National Theatre of Sarajevo. His life, like all citizens of Sarajevo, was changed in the early 1990s when war broke out. In 1992 a mortar shell fell on a crowd lined-up outside a bakery close to his home. Twenty-two people were killed. After that, she told them, he played in public. He played his cello in ruined buildings, he played in the outdoors, and he even played in danger from snipers.

"I don't know if it's true," Miss Fowler said, "but I have seen it reported that he was asked why he endangered himself by playing in dangerous settings to which he replied: 'You ask me am I crazy for playing the cello, why do you not ask if they are not crazy for shelling Sarajevo?'"

He became best known and admired around the world, Miss Fowler continued, for his performances of Albinoni's "Adagio in G Minor" which he played in the marketplace where the twenty-two people had been killed. "I think when I play it for you, you will understand why the citizens would have found it calming."

Miss Fowler then asked the class to paint what they imagined people living through the war felt when the heard the cello playing. While they painted, Miss Fowler played the Adagio. Melody was moved to tears.

As soon as she got home, Melody announced she was going to become a cellist and play the Adagio to make people feel good. Maybe, she said, she would play with the Met Orchestra. Since she did not waver from this over the next few months, Alison rented a cello and arranged for Melody to take lessons. She loved it and played endlessly. It was not long before she could, on warm evenings, take the cello over to the open apartment windows and play Albinoni's Adagio. She hoped that passers-by would enjoy it. Alison would sometimes stand and gaze at her daughter as she played. She looks like an angel, Alison thought, as Melody played, with her long blond hair framing her delicate face, and her big blue eyes reflecting her passion for the music.

When she finished high school, Melody was determined to follow her dreams and go to music school. She first considered Juillard. It was where Yo-Yo Ma had studied. But there were too many hurdles. The audition and interview did not bother her. But the acceptance rate was below ten percent, the cost of tuition was incredible, and there was a strong chance that in the year she would be ready to go, there would be no faculty member available for a cellist. She decided instead on the Manhattan School of Music. Perhaps it was not as prestigious as Juillard, but it had a good reputation and offered exactly what she wanted. If accepted, Melody could first do a Bachelor of Music and then a Master's with a focus on orchestral performance. Simon and Alison agreed with her choice. They were proud of her. No one was surprised, but everyone was ecstatic, when Melody got her acceptance letter.

With both children settled into university life, Simon and Alison spent more time on their research and were freer to travel to conferences. After they each secured tenure, they worked together to jointly research the backgrounds of malevolent leaders. Simon examined the socio-political contexts, and Alison researched the family and parenting factors. It was a good partnership. They found themselves in demand as keynote speakers at many international conferences, and guest lecturers at a variety of universities. They also attracted substantial research funding which allowed them extensive travel in Europe.

Michael had settled on the University of Toronto for his degrees. He liked their program, and he had enjoyed the city when he was there for a brief time during one of his debating trips. He loved that the campus and the student housing were almost in the city centre. Markets were within walking distance, and the cheap but delicious lunches on Spadina Avenue were just a few minutes away from the campus. Simon and Alison approved his choice since it was a relatively easy drive for them to visit, and a safe city for Michael to experience living away from home for the first time.

* * *

Melody met James during her first year at music school. They soon became inseparable, taking classes together, playing duets—some of their own composing—and going for long walks in Central Park. James' family was in Oregon, so he stayed in New York and spent Christmas with the Leelands. It was a magical time. New York was at its movie best. Snow blanketed the streets. The lights on the massive Christmas tree at Rockefeller Center twinkled, the skaters in colourful coats and scarves circled at the tree's base, and all around them store windows were full of dazzling Christmas displays and decorations.

Melody and James celebrated their engagement the night of Melody's twenty-first birthday in May of 1998. James' family was in the city to be present at his graduation, and Michael had come home from Toronto, where he was now working on a PhD in international relations, to introduce his Canadian girlfriend Amy to the family. It was the first and only evening the families were together.

The evening started with introductions, the engagement announcement, and drinks and appetizers in the Leelands' living room. James then surprised Melody by telling her that he had made reservations at the 21 Club for a late dinner. Michael and Amy and the two sets of parents decided to order in and have a relaxed evening getting to know each other. They settled on gourmet pizza.

While most of the family were enjoying beer and pizza, James and Melody sipped champagne, and then lingered over a wonderful steak dinner. They shared a crème brûlée for dessert. Leaving the restaurant, they were full, content, and radiating happiness. Life was perfect. On the sidewalk, they stopped for a moment and hugged each other. With hands clasped tightly they strolled down 52nd to 5th Avenue and stepped onto the crosswalk. A silver sports car sped toward them. Cries of "look out!" from other pedestrians were of no use. The car knocked Melody away from James. She landed on the hood of the car, then fell onto the road as the driver careened away. Melody died from her injuries at the hospital an hour later.

5

Alison and Simon

The families had finished their pizza and were enjoying a glass of port when there was a knock at the door. None could have imagined what they were about to learn. They did not get to the hospital in time to say goodbyes. The next few hours were a blur for Alison and Simon. They were in shock and feeling disconnected from reality. Later they were consumed by rage and loss.

They learned that James had been admitted into the psychiatric wing where he was sedated and watched for fear of suicide. And they learned later that the driver did not stop.

Rather than stopping after hitting Melody, the driver had sped off. Police quickly traced the car and driver. The exotic sports car was easily recognized, and there had been several witnesses to the crash who reported that the driver looked like a young woman with bright red hair. The investigating officer had a hunch who the driver might be.

She was right. The driver was the only daughter of a family who were known to skirt laws. It was eighteen-year-old heiress Samantha Costner, whose father was a well-known real estate developer in the city and reputed to be a money-laundering billionaire.

Because the police found Samantha within three hours, they could administer and use the results of a blood alcohol test. She failed it. They checked the car and found marks on the left side front fender that were consistent with hitting a person. The guilt seemed obvious.

During the police interview, Samantha explained she had spent most of the day shopping. "Sure, I stopped at the bar after. I was meeting a friend and I was exhausted from trying so much stuff on," Samantha whined, "but I only had one small drink. No way was I drunk, and no way did I hit anyone. I just came home. It wasn't me. Nope, no way, couldn't have been." She was charged.

Her father hired a team of lawyers who, eventually, conceded that it could have been Samantha driving the car that had hit the young woman. And they agreed she may have been impaired. But they also argued that she had been unaware that she was impaired. They insisted she was telling the truth when she said she had only one drink.

"The fact of the matter is that Ms. Costner had taken a pain killer for a headache just before she met her friend at the bar," the lawyer explained. "She couldn't possibly have known that she might be inebriated. She couldn't have known that the pain pill she took could amplify the effects of the alcohol. She's just a kid, a kid who made a mistake." Furthermore, they contended, she had owned the car for only two days. It was a birthday gift from her father, and she had driven it only once before. She had learned to drive on her mother's luxury sedan. She was unaccustomed to the sports car's powerful acceleration and handling.

"And," they added most egregiously, "the so-called victim here had been drinking. It seems plausible that she could have not looked before she stepped onto the crosswalk. She could well have stepped right into the path of Ms. Costner's car." A trial was ordered. In the meantime, Samantha was allowed to live at home, and ordered not to drive.

The trial dragged out over the next sixteen months and only maintained, if not intensified the sense of loss felt by Simon, Alison, Michael, and James. There were multiple court hearings. Samantha's father was skilled in prolonging the case. He arranged for expert witnesses. His lawyers repeatedly argued over test results. Overseas mechanics were called to describe how difficult it would have been for Samantha to handle the car well until she had time to get used to it. Character witnesses and Costner family members provided glowing reports about Samantha.

During each hearing, Samantha herself appeared arrogant and disinterested. She sat with the team of lawyers looking bored and devoid of emotion. Even when the victim impact statements were presented in court, she sat stoically, unaffected by the words that left others in the courtroom in tears. At no time did she admit any responsibility or apologize. Eventually, she received a $1,000 fine, and her licence was revoked for six months, a common response to a simple DWI.

Simon and Alison were too emotionally exhausted to appeal. They had been consumed by the trial for too long. By the time of the verdict, Simon and Alison were depleted and alone. James had moved back to Oregon with his family, and Michael and Amy had left for an extended backpacking trip to

Africa. It was time to move on, but the rage at the loss and the injustice remained simmering under the surface. It never left.

Moving on for Simon and Alison meant becoming absorbed in their teaching and research. Their colleagues and the administration were supportive, particularly since they both were becoming well-known experts in their fields. Over the next few years, with generous funding from the university research department, Simon and Alison travelled extensively. It helped them deal with their loss. They gave talks at universities in parts of Europe including Munich, Vienna, Amsterdam, and Berlin. They added a few days at the end of each trip to allow them to see the sights.

The sightseeing was often related to Simon's growing obsession with all things Hitler. In Munich they spent hours at the documentation centre. After the conference in Vienna, they went on a day trip to Mauthausen concentration camp. It was a day that was both enriching and gruelling. In Amsterdam they visited Anne Frank's house. For Alison, that was the most moving and memorable. Remembering what Anne had written in her diary, "I still believe, in spite of everything, that people are really good at heart," as she walked into the small and claustrophobic attic in which the family hid, Alison could not hold back the tears. And she cried again when they visited the Berlin Wall memorial and the Topography of Terror history museum.

Each trip raised so many questions for Alison. What made Anne Frank so hopeful? What drove Himmler to organize the mass murder of the Jews? His mother was known as a devout Catholic, his family was middle class, and he did well at school. Alison just didn't understand. Simon also was sad and full of questions. Why did we not learn from the Armenian genocide, what have we learned from the Holocaust? How did the world allow Pol Pot to kill millions of people in Cambodia? Their questions drove their research. The trips were not only educational and interesting, but also the shared experiences also put their loss in perspective. But nothing lessened the rage they felt toward Samantha.

6

Nigel

Lord Nigel Smythe II looked at himself in the full-length mirror in the changing room. He looked good in his tux. But he felt nothing but dread. He would soon be a married man. He reached for the glass of champagne on the bureau beside him and took a long drink.

"Are you going to be okay?" his friend Lucas asked.

"I have to be Luke, it's too late to back out. I have to be." Nigel sighed.

From the great room, where the families and friends were gathered, came the sound of the bagpipes. Nigel knew what that meant. In five minutes, he must stand at the makeshift altar. He must say "I do" when every part of him was shrieking "I can't."

"Luke," Nigel turned to his friend, "I have to do this. I have to go in there now." He took a step toward Lucas who responded by pulling Nigel into a tight hug. Nigel clung to him for a moment, then took a deep breath, and walked toward his future.

How had he come to this place, he asked himself.

Nigel had met his about to be wife, Karen Wilson, during his last year at Oxford University. He was sipping a latte between classes in crowded cafeteria. He looked up and noticed a face that looked vaguely familiar. The woman was searching for a seat. Then, flipping back her elegantly coiffed blond hair, she had walked over to his table.

"May I share this table with you?" she had asked Nigel.

"Please," he'd responded, standing up and pulling out the empty chair for her to sit.

"Thank you. I'm Karen Wilson." He recalled her then. The only daughter of Baron and Lady Wilson, well-known patrons of the theatre in London.

Karen later told him that she thought he looked a lot like Sean Connery: tall, dark, and handsome, though not quite as muscular. While introducing herself, she had expected him to respond with "Bond, James Bond."

"Are you reading literature?" she had asked looking at the copy of James Joyce's *Dubliners* that was on the table.

Ever the well-bred gentleman, Nigel had closed the book and turned his attention to Karen. As they talked, he had discovered that like him, she was reading English literature, and had aspirations to be a writer. They'd had a long discussion about their professors and the books they were reading, and agreed to meet for coffee again.

Nigel had found her passion for literature and intelligence appealing. Although Nigel had felt no physical attraction to Karen, he had enjoyed her company. It seemed to him that she shared all his interests, and over the next few months they spent many hours together discussing books over coffee, going to plays and movies, and hiking through the countryside. As their friendship developed, she occasionally suggested he stay overnight at her flat. She seemed surprised that he had never agreed to do so, but Karen never really pushed the issue and never questioned why he did not want to make love. Perhaps if she had, he thought to himself, things would be different now.

Nigel recalled how happy his parents were when they met Karen. She was, they had told Nigel, everything they had dreamed of in a daughter-in-law and future mother of their grandchildren. She had, they said, just the right pedigree. They had urged Nigel to marry her and settle down. Another chance to stop the trajectory of the relationship, he thought. Why didn't I just say no? But setting aside his true feelings had proven too difficult. Ignoring the loud warning voices in his head, Nigel gave in to his parents' demands and Karen's obvious wishes to become Lady Smythe the younger. Now, only eight months after they first met, the time had come. Head held high, and ever the dutiful son, he walked into the great room and took his place to await the bride.

* * *

Somehow, though sheer force of will and denial, Nigel managed to behave more or less as expected through the wedding ceremony and honeymoon. Once back at his estate, they settled into a comfortable married routine. It seemed like their relationship could work, but it soon became obvious that Karen had married him for his title and family wealth. She never finished her degree. Her apparent passion for literature was replaced with a passion for shopping. Her apparent aspiration to be a writer became an aspiration to redecorate. He soon realized that she was capricious, and that her interests were short-lived. The one thing that had not changed was her desire to be part of the Smythe family wealth and status.

"I want to have a baby," she announced one night.

"Why, are you bored?" Nigel couldn't resist asking.

"How can you be so horrid," she replied, "you know your parents want a grandchild more than anything. And I want a baby."

"But do you also want to raise a child?"

Karen walked out of the room, slamming the door. They remained angry and hardly spoke for the next few days, but Nigel was not comfortable living in a state of hostility.

"Karen, if you really want to have a baby, let's try. I think I'd make a good father and you were quite right that my parents would be thrilled."

The only true happiness for Nigel came when Karen announced she was pregnant and six months later when she gave birth to a robust and beautiful baby boy. They named him Harrison Stafford after each of their grandfathers. Nigel was ecstatic to have a son. His parents expressed their joy with gifts and a substantial investment in an education fund for Harrison. Karen enjoyed the attention and the gifts but was increasingly unhappy.

The family wealth and title were losing their glamour. Nigel bored her, and motherhood, she decided, was not for her. If she was going to be kept awake at night she thought, it should be because she was at a party or enjoying hot sex, not by a squalling stinky infant. Her restlessness grew.

"What is it you want?" Nigel asked in frustration one

night after Harrison fell asleep. "You complain all the time. Nothing is ever enough for you is it. We've been married for less than two years, you have everything you want, we live in this magnificent estate, have a great lifestyle, and this amazing baby. I don't understand why you are so unhappy."

Karen stared at him for a moment and then stormed out. She returned very late at night and very drunk. From then on, things got worse.

The end came on the day that the London Tabloids published a photograph of a scantily clad Karen kissing a married member of parliament. *Politicians Behaving Badly*, the banner headline read. Scandal was not acceptable to the Smythes. Much to Nigel's relief, his parents used their money and influence to arrange for a quick and quiet divorce. Harrison would remain with Nigel. They were pleased, as was Nigel, when soon after the divorce, Karen left for New Zealand with her most recent lover, an older wealthy resort owner.

Embarrassed by the scandal, Nigel's parents left for a luxury guided safari in Botswana. They would be gone for six weeks. Long enough, they hoped, for the gossipers to find a new target. Seven days into their trip, Nigel's parents died in a plane crash. One reason they had chosen that particular safari was the use of light aircraft rather than jeeps to travel among the locations. The jeeps, they thought, would be too uncomfortable.

In a short period, Nigel had lost his wife and parents, and although he mourned the losses, he also felt liberated. As he entered his third decade of life, Nigel was free to be himself. Perhaps if same-sex marriage had been accepted when he was younger, he thought, he would not have been pressured to keep his sexual identity a secret from his family. Perhaps he would not have felt obliged to marry a woman in order to make his parents happy and provide them with the heir they so longed for. Perhaps he would not have so readily been duped by a would-be heiress. But the future was his. He decided that, at least for a while, he would enjoy casual sex but avoid any emotionally intimate relationships. Caring for Harrison became the most important part of Nigel's life, and the greatest joy he had ever experienced. He was completely comfortable and happy being a gay single dad.

The inheritance Nigel received from his parents, together with the travel and life insurance payments from his parents' deaths, allowed Nigel to be a full-time father. Through the preschool years, father and son spent many hours hiking, rowing on the Thames, and travelling down to Brighton Beach where Harrison would play for hours at the water's edge. Starting when Harrison was three, Nigel added monthly visits to either a museum or a concert to their activities. Harrison started school a happy, self-confident, and healthy child who was well prepared to excel.

They spent school holidays travelling. Nigel avoided taking Harrison to amusement parks, preferring instead to introduce him to iconic sights in Europe. When Harrison was six, Nigel took him to Venice. Harrison was enthralled with his first plane ride. The flight attendant, noticing the father with his look alike son, asked Harrison if he'd like to see the cockpit and say hello to the pilot.

"Can I daddy?" he asked, his eyes sparkling.

Five minutes later, an over-excited Harrison returned to his seat and chattered non-stop about the pilot and all the controls until they landed at Marco Polo Airport.

"Come on Harrison, let's get a taxi to our hotel." Nigel picked up their luggage and took Harrison's hand.

"Where are the taxis, daddy?" asked a puzzled Harrison. "I only see water and some boats."

"This is Venice, Harrison. We travel by water; there are canals and boats instead of roads and cars. And there are water buses and water taxis and special boats called gondolas. We'll take a ride on one." Nigel grinned at his son's quizzical expression.

After thirty minutes of rapid bouncing over the waves, father and son arrived at their hotel. An overtired and over stimulated Harrison fell asleep soon after they checked in. The trip was the first of their many adventures in Europe.

By age twelve, Harrison had seen much of Europe. In France, Nigel had taken him on a boat cruise down the Seine for lunch at the top of the Eiffel Tower. In Switzerland they had taken the Jungfrau train to the peak where they built a snowman, and in Paris, Munich, Amsterdam, and Vienna, Nigel and Harrison had attended concerts and museums. Harrison loved museums that had interactive exhibits, especially the Nemo Science Museum in Amsterdam. But the trip to Venice remained his favourite. Life seemed too good to be true.

Ian and Fiona

It was a typical spring day in Halifax. The temperature was barely above freezing, and the rain was heavy. The MacLean family was sitting around the kitchen table eating lunch and enjoying the warmth of the old wood stove. It was a family that seemed to be ever growing. On this day, at the table with Ian and Fiona were seven-year-old Lachlan, five-year-old Caitlin, and fifteen-month-old Maggie who sat in her high-chair.

"When is our new sister coming?" asked Lachlan.

"And will she play with me?" Caitlin added.

Fiona smiled at the children. "She'll be here very soon. But remember, we talked about how she may be feeling a bit sad or scared."

It had been almost ten years since Ian had agreed with Fiona that it would be good to foster and adopt rather than give birth. Since their marriage, they had fostered many children; they had adopted the three at the table today. Lachlan and Caitlin were siblings. They had been born to a single mother who died of an opioid overdose when they were one and three years old. Ian and Fiona had fostered them from the time of the overdose until they were four and two. They then applied to adopt the children. This was a decision they had never regretted. They adopted Maggie at birth in a private arrangement.

One of the teenage girls at the church had been raped by her boyfriend. Left pregnant, she sought counselling from Ian. She did not want to keep the baby, but she also did not want an abortion. She was uncertain about adoption, worrying about what sort of family her baby would grow up in. She was thrilled when Ian and Fiona offered to adopt the baby. They decided on an open adoption so that Maggie's birth family would become her extended family. Today, they were expecting their tenth foster child to arrive. She would be the oldest one to date, and perhaps the most difficult.

Fiona knew well that twelve-year-old Heather's history suggested that she would be the biggest challenge that she and Ian had yet faced as foster parents. Heather's mother had run away from an abusive home at age sixteen and soon found herself pregnant. With the help of a social worker, she planned to get a job and keep the baby, and she agreed to finish school on a part-time basis. It all sounded good until Heather was born. The time and care Heather needed was well beyond her mother's capacity, and by Heather's first birthday social workers had documented enough neglect that Heather was taken into foster care.

After four months in care, children's services returned Heather to her mother, who had taken parenting classes and tested clean for drug use. The reunion, like the drug-free state, was short-lived. Heather was removed again and placed with a second foster family. This pattern continued. Each separation and each upheaval added to Heather's distrust of adults, and her difficulties building relationships. By the time she came to join the MacLean clan, she had experienced twelve different family situations, many separated by a temporary stay with her biological mother, and she had attended five different schools. Not surprisingly, she had also developed several behaviour disorders, and was failing at school.

"You know Ian, I admit to being nervous, but I do think it'll work out, Are you confident?" Fiona asked, as they cleared the plates from the table.

"Well," replied Ian, "with God's help, we will provide Heather with stable and affectionate care, something I don't think she has ever experienced."

"I hope you're right. It'll be tough, but hey we'll do it—like the Beatles' song, 'All You Need Is Love.'" She leaned over and gave Ian a kiss. What she had not yet talked to Ian about was her determination that they would adopt Heather so that she would never have to change her family again.

The sound of tires on the gravel driveway attracted the family's attention. Looking out the kitchen window, Lachlan shouted, "They're here, mom! Our new sister is here!"

Lachlan's welcoming smile was not returned. A sullen, tall, thin, pale, and poorly dressed child stood on the porch, her stringy hair in need of a wash. She was clutching an old gym bag which held all her possessions. Lachlan was disappointed and thought she looked scary. Caitlin looked nervous and went and stood close to her father. Maggie carried on banging her spoon on the tray of the highchair.

To Fiona, Heather simply looked like a child in need of a

loving permanent home and family. Fiona smiled at her, and she and Ian welcomed Heather into her new home—her forever family, Fiona said. She introduced Heather to her new siblings, and then Fiona showed her to the room they had ready for her. Heather remained sullen and showed no interest in the other children, or the games and books they had provided for her. It was only when they gave her a tablet that her face lit up with joy. She sat on the bed clutching it to her chest. They left her to settle in.

Lachlan and Caitlin were full of questions.

"Why does she look so mean?"

"Why didn't she say hello?"

"Where's her other stuff?"

"Doesn't she want to be with us?"

Fiona sat on the sofa between the children with an arm around each of them.

"Remember," she said, "Heather's probably feeling pretty scared right now. She doesn't know us. She may think we will be mean to her like others have been. Remember we talked about how she had been in so many different homes and how her mom couldn't look after her properly. She's had a very tough time and you two will have to be very patient until she gets to know how wonderful you guys are. Okay?"

They did not see Heather again until dinner time. The other children watched in amazement as she struggled to use cutlery, grabbed her food with her fingers, and ate alarmingly quickly. She spoke to no one. Hasn't she ever had a dinner before, Lachlan wondered. Caitlin just stared unbelievingly. Maggie watched and giggled. After the meal, Heather grabbed some cookies and ran into her room. Fiona and Ian later went to say goodnight to her. She was sleeping on top of the bed wearing a raggedy old nightgown. The tablet was beside her. The cookies were nowhere to be seen. They assumed she had eaten them all.

Later the next day, Fiona discovered that Heather was hoarding food under her mattress. This child clearly has not been properly fed, Fiona thought, leaving the cookies where she found them. She knew that once Heather came to accept that food would always be available, she would no longer hoard it. In the meantime, the security of having a few snacks under the bed might be helpful. And she could sure use the calories, Fiona thought to herself. Fiona decided to check with Ian about the possibility of the food attracting mice before making a final decision.

In the meantime, they would go shopping and get the child some decent clothes and shoes. She would start another new school on Monday and Fiona was aware how important it was that Heather at least be dressed like the other children. She started a list: underwear, pajamas, jeans, T-shirts, sweatshirt, jacket, socks and runners. And, she decided, a decent haircut. She'd take Heather to the Mic Mac Mall in Dartmouth the next day. They could do all the shopping there, and maybe enjoy lunch at the food court. She checked that Ian was free to care for the other children, called the discount hair salon she used, and made an appointment for Heather. We are going to make this work, she told herself. But she was also wondering if Heather would even agree to go with her.

"What young girl wouldn't want a whole new wardrobe?"

Ian asked when Fiona expressed her concerns. "She's probably not had much other than hand-me-downs. She'll love it, you'll see."

Ian was wrong. The day was even worse than Fiona had thought possible. First Heather had refused to go, then she wouldn't try anything on. And she refused to have her hair cut. The only thing Heather agreed to was lunch. But there was no conversation, no relaxation. She ate a hotdog at record speed, and her bottle of soda pop was gone in two long noisy slurps. It was far from the shopping and lunch day that Fiona had hoped for.

Things didn't get any better for a long time. Heather was constantly testing the family's commitment to her by acting out, and she was not getting along with the children at home, or her classmates at school. Lachlan and Caitlin avoided her. Ian and Fiona did their best to remain calm and loving.

Justin

Justin knew that his first day with the split Grade 8 and 9 class would not be easy. He was right. "Hi," he introduced himself, to the twenty-six teens staring at him. "My name is Justin Marley. I'm your social studies teacher this year."

Hands shot up. "Ooh sir, are you related to Bob? You sorta look like him."

Justin smiled. "No but I do like his music." Handled that one, he thought.

"Are you from Jamaica sir?" "No, but my father was. I am here from Toronto."

"What about your mom?"

"She was from Thailand, but that's enough about me. Let's talk about what we will be discussing this semester."

"Sir, sir, would you please answer one more question?"

Sighing, Justin agreed. He wanted to establish a good rapport with his students. "But just one more."

"Sir, have you ever had a Brazilian wax?"

The class tittered. This I was not expecting, Justin thought to himself. Stay calm, stay calm. "Why do you ask?"

"Well sir, like I saw on Facebook that this guy said he wanted like a Brazilian, but the beauty salon wouldn't like do it. My dad said it's because they like don't do that for guys, but this one wanted it cos he was like transgender. I also heard that he was like so mad no one would do it that he like went to the Human Rights Commission—whatever that is. I wondered, sir, if you ever like thought about having your...."

"Why do you think he went to the Human Rights Commission," Justin interrupted. He would deal with the use of 'like' later.

"Don't know—how would we know? We don't have rights."

"Trans people have rights, don't they sir?"

"Yes, they do, but so do I, and so do you."

Justin seized the opportunity to move the conversation and told the class that they in fact did have rights under the UN Convention on the Rights of the Child. The rest of the class passed in a discussion of the nature of rights, and why they are important. Justin promised the class that over the next week they could research children's rights and look at issues such as how Conventions are developed, and what rights children and teens have.

Walking back to his studio apartment in Kitsilano at the end of the day, Justin decided he should celebrate having survived his first full day in a new school and particularly his handling of the Brazilian question. He was musing over how to celebrate as he walked into the lobby of his apartment building. At the mailboxes was his neighbour Jennifer. They had said hi and chatted briefly the previous week when they were both moving in. Jennifer was studying a pizza menu that had come with the day's mail.

Looking at Jennifer, Justin decided he did not want to celebrate alone. Looking at the pizza menu in her hand, he decided he deserved a celebratory dinner. He made a quick decision. "Hi Jennifer, nice to see you again."

"Oh," she replied looking up from the menu," hi, it's Justin, right?"

"Yup, and I have a great favour to ask of you. I just survived my first day of teaching in a new school with a class of rambunctious kids and I want to celebrate. Yesterday was great—just met the other staff, but today was a whole different experience. Would you consider having dinner with me? No strings attached. I just want to relax with an adult and talk about—no, laugh about—my day with the kids."

"I'd like that," Jennifer replied, after a brief hesitation. "I've been having way too much pizza. I was just looking at the takeout menu here and wondering if I could stomach another. Give me time for quick shower and I'll be ready. Where will we go? McDonalds?" she asked with a grin.

"Do you like jazz? Because this is Wednesday and at Provence Marinaside they have a jazz band on Wednesday evenings, and I've heard that the food there is terrific."

"Is the Pope Catholic?" Jennifer answered, smiling. "I love jazz, thank you."

"Great! Maybe we can get a table overlooking the harbour. You go shower, I'll see if I can get us a reservation. Let's meet here in thirty-five minutes. Is that okay?"

Justin had been told by his Toronto friends that it always rained in Vancouver. But so far, he had been lucky, and it was a glorious September evening. Justin decided that given the weather, it would be nice to walk down to Granville Island market and take the Aquabus ferry to Yaletown. The stop was pretty much at the restaurant. Jennifer was delighted. Like Justin, she had only moved to Vancouver a few weeks earlier and was keen to explore the area. They arrived at the restaurant in time for a magnificent view of the sunset set from their table. They were far enough from the trio who were playing smooth jazz to chat without yelling. Justin, watching Jennifer's long brown hair blowing softly in the breeze, and mesmerized by her large dark brown eyes, could not believe his luck.

As they enjoyed their food and wine, Justin told Jennifer about his first day. She was much amused by the Brazilian story and impressed with his handling of it. She was interested in learning that children had rights. Despite being a pediatric nurse, Jennifer had never come across issues of children's rights in her training. She was eager to learn more, particularly as many of the patients seemed to have had their rights denied. Jennifer described children who were malnourished, children with diabetes who had not received sufficient insulin, children who were sick because their parents were anti-vaxxers, and children suffering all kinds of injuries due to parental negligence or abuse. But not all the conversation was negative.

They shared stories of moving to Vancouver, apartment hunting, and their current apartments. Jennifer had moved from Quesnel to study at the University of British Columbia, hoping to make the city her permanent home. After graduation, she got a job at BC Children's Hospital, a job she loved. Justin noticed she said little about her life before the move and seemed to avoid talking about her family. In response to Justin's question, Jennifer acknowledged that her parents still lived in Quesnel, but then quickly changed the subject. Justin enjoyed talking about his own family, a large and happy mixed-race family with relatives in the Caribbean and Asia.

"If we ever had a real family reunion, we'd have to hire an arena," Justin said. "There are my parents, my three sisters, and two brothers in the Toronto area. There are grandparents in Jamaica and Thailand. I've never even met the ones in Thailand or many of the others. There are so many cousins, aunts, and uncles in both countries, as well as in Vietnam, Malaysia, and St. Lucia, that we've lost count."

Jennifer smiled, but Justin noted her posture stiffen when he mentioned uncles. Her mood seemed to change also. She put her napkin down and picked up her purse.

"This has been a great evening," Jennifer said. "I was expecting to have pizza and TV. This meal and the music have been wonderful. Thanks so much for including me in your celebration."

"The band is still playing. Shall we order another bottle of wine before we leave?"

"I have to be at the hospital by seven tomorrow so I probably shouldn't," replied Jennifer, "I should get home. But thanks."

Justin, registering her discomfort, asked their server for the bill and insisted on the evening being his treat. As they left the restaurant, the Aquabus ferry was just pulling up to the wharf. Going back across False Creek, they looked back at the twinkling multicoloured lights of Science World. Looking at the lights and listening to the sound of the boat and its wash, Jennifer visibly relaxed.

"I so love being here." Jennifer sighed. "I don't ever want to live anywhere else."

"Me too. I will happily put up with questions about Brazilian waxes and sexual identity if I can stay living and working here. Thanks so much for coming with me tonight. It's been cathartic and magical. I sure hope we can do it, or maybe McDonalds, again sometime."

They walked in companionable silence through the market area and along Fourth Avenue. Arriving back at their building, Justin walked Jennifer to her door where he gave Jennifer a brief hug and kissed her cheek as he wished her goodnight.

"Oh sorry," he said, as she flinched. "I didn't mean to upset you."

"It's okay," Jennifer replied looking uncomfortable, "I'm sorry, it's just that...."

"No need for explanations, thanks again for coming, have a good sleep. Good night."

Did I read that so wrong, Justin asked himself, as he got ready for bed. We had a great evening, and it was just a friendly hug. Exhausted, he fell into bed and slept through until the alarm at seven the next morning. Upon waking he was delighted that his dreams had been about jazz and boats, and nothing Brazilian.

Despite her hesitations that first night, Justin asked her out again a few days later, and much faster than he expected, they were spending almost every evening together. They quickly fell into a routine of taking turns to prepare dinner, and more often than not, Jennifer stayed overnight.

"My beautiful Jennifer," Justin said several weeks later after they had made love for the second time that evening, "would you consider moving in with me? We are spending most of our time together here, I have all this space and I adore you."

Since her apartment was a sublet, it had come furnished so there was no issue of whose furniture to keep. Besides, she would have chosen Justin's décor over hers anyway. His place was minimalist with simple pieces in white and pale grey. The only decorations were plants and a few paintings. She loved the calm, almost Zen-like, feel. He did not have a spare study for her, but she was insisted she did not need one. She let her landlord know, and at the end of the month moved her personal items into Justin's. Their lives meshed as easily as their belongings.

Over Christmas, Justin took Jennifer to Toronto to meet his parents. It was Jennifer's first time outside of British Columbia, and her first time on a plane larger than the Dash 8 on which she had flown to Vancouver from Quesnel. She was apprehensive about the trip and meeting Justin's family. But, although she was nervous on the way there, she quickly relaxed with the big friendly family. They gave her a warm welcome. The house was spacious, and it helped that they were quite happy for Jennifer to stay in Justin's room, and that it had an en-suite bathroom.

Justin's parents regaled her with stories and baby pictures of Justin, teasing him mercilessly. They proudly showed her their neighbourhood, and the city, and cooked massive quantities of Jamaican food which was shared with an endless stream of family members and friends. The love and laughter that accompanied all the outings and the meals left Jennifer feeling like she was a valued member of a family. It was a first for her. Justin wondered if she felt overwhelmed, especially when his parents expressed their delight with her joining their family and asked when the wedding would be.

Justin

Jennifer and Justin spent ten days with his parents. They left with many wonderful memories and lots of recipes. Jennifer had never tasted Jamaican food before but fell in love with its sweetness and the spices. She wanted to treat Justin one day to some jerk chicken with rice and peas for dinner. She had been surprised when Justin's mom served it to learn that the 'peas' in the recipe were actually red kidney beans. And she wanted to make him some bammy for breakfast. They had eaten that a few times and Jennifer absolutely loved it. She thought it was a bread but when she read the recipe, she found it was a vegetable: grated cassava root that was made into a bread like substance, dipped in coconut milk, and fried. The family also insisted that she take the recipe for ackee and codfish. It was the one thing she had tried that she did not like, but she politely and gratefully accepted it. Perhaps she would try again someday because it was clear to her that Justin had missed his mom's cooking.

On the flight back to Vancouver, Justin asked when he could meet her family. She changed the subject. She later admitted that she had no intentions of introducing him, or even letting them know of his existence. Being with him and being part of his family was all she wanted.

"Couldn't you at least let them we are living together?" he asked.

"No, and please Justin, don't push it."

"Is it the colour of my skin? My dreads?"

"Justin, God no," she insisted, "but I just don't want to talk about it. I love you, that's what matters."

After the Christmas break, Justin's classes became increasingly enjoyable. Telling his students about their rights under the Convention on the Rights of the Child and allowing them to exercise their participation rights in the classroom had resulted in the students responding to him with a great deal of respect and affection. It was an ideal environment for teaching and learning, and Justin felt fulfilled as a teacher. He felt even more content and fortunate to be with Jennifer. She was his dream partner, and he felt secure in her love for him. Life, he decided, was perfect.

Jennifer was happy also. She stayed in contact with Justin's parents, and delighted in telling them she had made a batch of bammy for Justin one Saturday morning. For the first time in her life, Jennifer felt a sense of belonging and fulfillment. She could not believe someone as wonderful as Justin loved her. She was scared it would not last but was determined to enjoy being part of his life and his world while it did. Nursing was also going well. Jennifer was working only day shifts in the pediatric oncology ward, which was her preference. She came home thrilled when a child went into remission, and even more so when the child was well enough to go home. And many did. But that was not always the case.

Against all her training and advice, Jennifer became emotionally attached to a new patient. Claire was a beautiful three-year-old who had been diagnosed with leukemia over Christmas. Claire's family lived in Kamloops, and although her mother came down to Vancouver as often as she could, she was the sole parent and sole supporter, so it was difficult. It was no hardship for Jennifer to spend extra time with Claire; she enjoyed reading her stories and singing to her. She happily gave up her break times to be with Claire, and sometimes stayed an extra hour at the end of the day to make sure Claire was okay before her sleep time. After a few months of treatment, Claire was recovering well, like so many young children with leukemia.

The morning before the Easter weekend, Jennifer arrived with a new book for Claire. The room was empty. Late the previous evening, Claire had taken a sudden and unexpected turn for the worse. The head nurse told Jennifer that Claire died before morning. Jennifer, distraught, ran from the hospital.

* * *

Justin called Jennifer's name as he entered their apartment that night and was surprised by the silence. Jennifer was usually home before him on Thursdays, and it was her turn to cook dinner. He was hoping she had made jerk chicken. But the luring aromas that usually filled the apartment were absent. Odd, thought Justin, her coat and boots are here. He called again. Wondering where she was, Justin decided to get changed and then call her on her cell. Maybe she had stayed later with Claire, he thought. What he saw when he went into their bedroom to change was permanently seared on his brain.

Jennifer was lying on the bed, a note by one hand and an empty pill bottle by the other. She was white. Justin was too late. Her body was cold and the CPR he desperately tried was ineffective. He called 911 and then picked up the note.

Dear Justin,

I realized today that I am not worthy of you or the happiness I feel when we are together. I had hoped to be good enough but I guess I knew all along that I'm not.

I am a failure. I have always been a misfit and a failure. I let Claire die Justin. That beautiful little girl, Claire is dead. I should have saved her. I should be the dead one, not that innocent child. I can't do anything right. I have known that for years. My mom told me I was a mistake; she never wanted a kid. She said it would have been okay if I'd been a boy, but I was just an ugly and stupid little girl who was ruining her life. My Uncle Ray also told me I'd never be worthy of love — that's why he needed to fuck me — to force himself on me. Oh did it hurt — it hurt my body and it hurt my soul Justin. Night after night he came into my bed and stuck his penis in my vagina and in my mouth until I gagged and gagged — I was just a little girl Justin, 7 years old. I told my mom and she said to stop making things up, if he wants you you're lucky, she said, no-one else would ever want you, you are ugly and useless and stupid. You will always be a failure. You should never have been born. They were right Justin, I am no good. I am a failure. I could not save Claire, I am afraid I will hurt you. I love you too much to hurt you. I should not have been born. I was and I am a mistake. You're too good for me, you are so wonderful you deserve...

Here the letter petered out. Justin's screams brought the neighbours, and then the police to the door.

10

Ian and Fiona

Fiona had expected the adjustment period to be difficult, but it was even worse than she had thought possible. It was over a year before Heather calmed down and accepted that she was not going to be sent away again. Once she trusted she was safe, she paid more attention and worked harder at school, and was friendlier with the other children. Her behaviour and relationships might have continued to improve had the social workers not decided that since her biological mother was clean again, Heather should start spending some time with her. Bi-monthly weekend visits were scheduled to start immediately with the intent of moving to weekly as soon as feasible.

Ian and Fiona objected but were over-ridden by a strong policy of family reunification. For reasons Ian and Fiona could not understand, the policy assumed that the most important thing for children was to be with their biological parents.

What the social workers did not know was that Heather's biological mother, Diane, was involved with a man, Alexander Santos, who had a history of internet child luring. He also had been convicted of, and served a short sentence for, producing and distributing child sexual abuse images. Either Diane had cleverly kept his presence in her life a secret, or the social workers had not done their jobs.

The first few visits passed without incident. Heather had never been consulted about spending weekends with her biological mother and showed little interest in doing so. She went reluctantly but without acting out before or after the weekends with them. Then Heather began misbehaving on the day or evening before a scheduled visit. She would pick fights at school, be cruel to the neighbour's cat, and twice she lit fires in the house. One fire she lit in the garbage can in the kitchen, the other under the mattress on her bed. On both occasions, Ian noticed and was able to quickly douse the fires.

Neither Ian nor Fiona got angry with Heather. Fiona realized that her behaviour reflected how intensely she did not want to spend the weekend with her mother. But she did not know why. After the younger children went to bed one evening, Ian and Fiona called Heather into the living room.

"Heather, we are wondering if you would rather not go to your mom's this weekend," Fiona asked her.

"Whatever."

"You know if it upsets you to go there, you don't have to go," Ian explained.

Heather shrugged. "I'm tired, I'm going to my room." She left the living room.

"I'm sure something's up, Ian. But whatever it is, she isn't going to tell us, is she."

Discussing their concerns further, Ian and Fiona decided they would call Heather's case worker, Susan Wright, in the morning, fill her in, and see if she'd help.

Susan returned their call late that afternoon. Fiona explained her concerns.

"Heather," she said, "has behaved in ways that suggest something is happening on the visits to her mother that is really upsetting her. She behaves badly before the visit, and she comes back sullen, angry, and aggressive. We've tried talking with her, but she'll tell us nothing. We were hoping that you could check the situation to see if she—."

"Look, Mrs. MacLean," Susan interrupted Fiona. "I'm sorry, but I must remind you I have thirty children in my caseload right now, not just Heather."

"I know what it's like. Our office is swamped, too."

"Well, as I have told you a number of times now, we are monitoring her mother as best we can. She is clean, and we have seen no evidence of maltreatment. Heather's just acting like a teenager, that's all. I have to go now, I have a client waiting." The call ended.

Fiona was furious. Both she and Ian were convinced something was happening on those visits that was deeply disturbing to Heather. It was not until much later that they learned the full story.

Alexander, although well hidden from social workers, was always present during Heather's visits. Diane often left the two of them alone. At first, Alexander was charming and friendly with Heather. He showed her a lot of positive attention, telling her she was pretty, asking her how she got so smart, and playing computer games with her. He also bought her gifts, including, one day, an iPhone. She was thrilled. He seemed to be everything Heather had wished for in a father.

He was, Heather thought, a lot more fun than Ian. She loved spending time with Alexander and was happy her mom went out and left the two of them together. That didn't last. Alexander had a plan which he masterfully executed. Once he was sure he had Heather's trust, he was ready to move on to step two: the introduction of sexual content into their games and conversation.

It started with Alexander saying she looked so beautiful that he wanted her to pose for a couple of photos. He told her he had a new camera he was learning to use, and it would really help him if she'd be his model. Heather, flattered, did not hesitate to pose for him. Over the next few visits, the poses and the photos became increasingly sexualized. Heather had no difficulty complying with his requests which were still in her comfort zone. She enjoyed the attention, and she thought the sexy poses were fun.

The first time she felt queasy was when he asked her to bare her newly formed breasts for the camera. She hesitated, but he assured her no one else would see the photos, he wouldn't even show them to her mom. They were just for him because he knew she was very special.

"And anyway," he continued, "you know you are pretty enough to be in the movies. Don't you want to be a star? This is how they start."

She obeyed. After she got dressed and Alexander had left, she considered talking to her mother who had just come home after a shopping trip. But she dismissed the idea. She did not want to risk what she perceived to be the good relationship she had with Alexander. She had liked his explanation but was not really sure that it was okay. What harm could it do, she thought, just this once? They were just having fun, and he was just learning how to take different shots with his camera. She decided she would not go topless again. That made her feel better. But at the next visit, when Diane was out again, Alexander insisted on more topless shots. When she hesitated, he threatened her with releasing the pictures and telling her foster parents she was being inappropriate. Scared, she complied.

Over the next few months, Alexander became more demanding with Heather. He coerced her into removing more and more of her clothing and adopting increasingly suggestive poses. At each visit he promised it would not go further. At each visit the photos became more explicit. Eventually he threatened to distribute the sexual images he had of her online for all to see unless she complied with further sexual activity. She wanted to tell Fiona and Ian, but she was afraid that they would hate her for what she had done and kick her out. But she could not bring herself to comply with Alexander's demands.

When she refused to allow more pictures, he did as he had threatened. He posted mages of an almost fully nude Heather on multiple porn sites and social media, tagged with her name and city. It was not long before her peers at school saw them. The resultant bullying was unendurable.

Before Ian and Fiona could step in, Heather ran away. It was only then that Ian and Fiona learned the truth about Heather's reluctance to visit her biological mother. In an unannounced visit to Diane, Susan Wright had discovered

Alexander, and suspected what had happened. She apologized to Ian and Fiona. Soon afterwards, she resigned her position. But the damage had been done.

11

Alison and Simon

"Did you know that another difference between Hitler and Trump was that Hitler didn't eat cheeseburgers," Simon explained, as Alison took a large bite of her juicy burger. "Hitler was vegetarian."

Had Simon always been so obsessed with Hitler, Alison wondered. Certainly not when they first met thirty-six years ago.

"Do you remember, Simon, that the first time we came here for a meal was to celebrate Melody's acceptance to the Manhattan School of Music?" Thinking of Melody, Alison put down her hamburger and wiped a tear from her eye. Time had not healed her pain.

"Yea, we were all so full of hope for her. What an amazing future she would have had."

They looked silently at each other for a few moments.

Alison took a sip. "Remember when Melody first met James? I have never seen anyone's eyes sparkle like hers did."

"What I remember is how wonderfully they played together. James on his sax and Melody on her cello. It was such a different sound, hauntingly beautiful."

He turned to Alison, "Let's drink a toast to those days."

"How's the burger? Can I get you another drink?" The questions brought them back to the present.

"Thanks, the burger's great and yes, I'll have another Bellini."

Simon smiled at Alison, "You must be the only woman whose favourite meal is a burger with Bellinis. We could have gone out for steak tonight. Who else celebrates their thirtieth anniversary at a place like this?"

"Yea, what a thirty years it's been. Cheers!" Alison raised her glass before sipping the icy drink.

"Cheers! You remember when we met, I had long brown curly hair and a beard."

Alison laughed, "Did you ever. Remember when we were looking for an apartment and that guy said you looked like that murderer—I forget his name."

"You mean Charles Manson?" Simon asked.

"Yea, that's the one. That was pretty funny. It's a good thing we didn't like that apartment. Now you just look like everyone's image of Einstein. And I have been sagging and bagging over the years. Sometimes I see my reflection in a store window, and I wonder who the old lady is."

"But you still look beautiful to me, and we still love each other, right?"

"More than ever."

They finished their meal in silence, each absorbed in memories of their past.

The server cleared their plates. "Can I bring you some dessert? Tonight, we are featuring cheesecake, tiramisu, a cheese plate, or a chocolate ganache truffle."

"Calories be damned," grinned Alison, "I'll have the truffle."

"And I the tiramisu. Oh, and would you please bring each of us a coffee and a Kahlua."

"You know," Simon said, turning back to Alison, "that's another common Hitler and Trump thing—no alcohol. But it's our anniversary. Can't stop with Bellinis. We may as well live it up. Oh man, here's your truffle. It looks amazing."

"Remember how Melody loved chocolate," Alison sighed.

Simon stretched across the table and took her hand in his. "It's okay to still be sad babe. I am too. Still sad, and still very angry."

"More coffee? Another liquor?"

"Coffee please."

"Me too. Thanks."

"I hope you enjoyed your meal. Take the bill to the front to pay when you are ready. No rush. Do you have anything special planned for the rest of the evening?"

Simon grinned, "Yes, but nothing we should discuss in public."

Holding hands, they left the restaurant and began the mile walk back to their apartment.

"I have an idea," Simon said, as they strolled along. "We both have a sabbatical leave coming up in January. We'll have nine whole months without classes, and there's really no reason for us to stay in New York all the time. Think about this Mrs. Leeland: we've had thirty years together."

"Actually it's thirty-six, if you count living in sin," Alison interrupted, laughing.

"I stand corrected. Do you realize that in all that time, those thirty-six years, thirty-six not thirty years," Simon stressed good humoredly, "we have never taken a real holiday? Sure, we've had lot of trips, but they've always been work related. And think of the loyalty points we must have. We could probably travel free. Imagine just the two of us, going somewhere just for fun."

"Are you suggesting what I think you are? A real vacation? Am I hearing you right? Do you actually mean there'd be no visits to concentration camps, no Nazi documentation centres, and no talk of Trump? If so, I'm all for it."

"I promise. We'll go somewhere we have never been before, and we'll just read novels."

"But not those set in the Second World War," interrupted Alison with a grin.

"And we'll walk beaches."

"And have little paper umbrellas in all our drinks."

"Yes, absolutely umbrellas. We deserve a special break. We've had a lot of stress. Let's just go somewhere and be kids again with no worries."

The discussion continued. By the time they arrived home, they had settled on Asia, a continent to which they had never travelled, and to the best of their knowledge neither had Hitler. They did a computer search of popular places in Asia. Thailand looked most appealing to them. It was relatively inexpensive which was one consideration. Various travel sites described it as having a rich history and culture as well as great beaches, warm weather, friendly people, and delicious food.

"Sounds idyllic," Alison said. "Let's check out the beaches."

Google search informed them of the best beach destinations. They dismissed locations such as Pattaya, Ko Samui, and Pa Tong, because they did not want a lively area with nightlife. That left Phuket as the most attractive option. They picked the top-rated resort on Karon Beach in Phuket and made a reservation before either of them could change their mind. Alison suggested they go for two weeks. Ignoring her, Simon made the reservation for four weeks.

Although neither had said so, they each hoped that the month on the beach in Thailand would be healing. Twenty years was more than enough time to carry the intense sadness and rage they still felt at the loss of Melody. At the very least it would be a novel experience for them, and a chance to create new memories. When they were not walking on the beach, they planned to spend much of their time reading by the pool. They had noticed that the resort offered classes in tai chi and Buddhism. Both were appealing. Simon had read online that the Mayo Clinic recommended tai chi for stress reduction. That should help. They also hoped that the Buddhist meditation practices would help them achieve calm. Enlightenment seemed too grand a goal.

Justin

Justin was paralyzed with grief. As soon as his parents heard what happened, they flew from Toronto to be with him and to attend the memorial service. They ended up staying for five weeks to take care of him, and to help him adjust to his loss. His students and colleagues hoped he would return after a period of mourning, but he remained unable to do so. The school hired a substitute teacher to finish the year.

Justin had no memories of Jennifer's memorial service although he knew he had attended. He was aware that no one from Jennifer's family had attended. Weeks passed with Justin avoiding talking, not eating, using sedatives, and staying in bed. Deeply concerned about his mental health, his mother arranged for a therapist. Looking through reviews online she identified a Dr. Jane Miles whose office was nearby, and who had excellent reviews for grief counselling. She arranged for Justin to see Dr. Miles and paid for fifteen sessions in advance. It was difficult getting Justin to agree to go, but he was eventually worn down by her insistence.

It took Justin four months of weekly counselling before he could remove Jennifer's belongings from his apartment. His mother, who had been phoning him daily, returned to Vancouver to help him. She was relieved to see that he was off all medication. Together they packed up Jennifer's clothing and donated it to the local Salvation Army thrift shop. Before she left, his mother filled Justin's freezer with the home cooked meals he had enjoyed as a child. With his mother's return to Toronto, and with all of Jennifer's possessions gone, Justin no longer felt at home in his apartment. He was not sure where he wanted to go, or what he wanted to do. All he knew for sure is that he could not return to teaching in the fall.

During his next two sessions with Dr. Miles, Justin explored his options. She agreed that moving on required that he resign his teaching position, take a break, and then move to a different area if he still felt the same way. One of the other teachers at his school heard that Justin was planning to move out of his apartment and offered him the use of his basement suite for a three-month period.

"You might as well use it, Justin. Our current tenants are moving out next week, and we have a niece who's going to move in while she goes to university here. She won't be here until January."

"If you're sure, I'd love that. I'm not sure how long I'll stay, I want to get right away for a while, but if I can stay with you until I sort things out, that'd be really helpful."

The move was easy. The house was in the same neighbourhood, and Justin had sold or given away what he owned other than a few books, some CDs, and his clothes. He needed to feel he could leave at any moment with nothing more than a backpack for his possessions. He called his parents to give them his new address.

"You know, Justin," his mother said. "We have been thinking that this might be the ideal time for you to visit your ancestral homeland. Travel around and meet your Thai relatives. Take a year or so and then decide what you want to do."

His mother had fond memories of her Thai roots and culture. She had always encouraged him to learn about his Thai ancestry, and always hoped that he would have the opportunity to go to Thailand. This seemed like the time. It would provide distraction, and there were several family members there if Justin needed support. Justin agreed with his mother that it would be good to get to know the Thai side of his ancestry. He knew he had an aunt in Bangkok, and other relatives around, but he could not imagine meeting them now. Maybe after some time alone, he said. But the more he thought about going to Thailand, the more it seemed like a good idea. What appealed to him most about going there was what he remembered about the Buddhism and meditation practices his family had talked about, and practised, when he was growing up.

He remembered his mother giving him books about Thai culture and religion. Much to his annoyance as a teenager, she would quiz him about what he had learned. But perhaps because of that, he still remembered reading that Thailand was the largest Buddhist country in the world with over ninety percent of Thais practising the religion. It had meant little to him as a teenager, but it particularly appealed to him in his current circumstances that most Thais practised Theravada Buddhism. Theravada Buddhism, he recalled, encouraged the use of meditation to solve problems, to understand the true nature of things, and to calm the mind. Exactly what he needed, he thought. Justin also liked the idea of some time alone at a place where he could just walk on a beach, somewhere quiet and restful. He decided his mother was right. He would go to Thailand.

Justin looked through the Tripadvisor travel service to identify some options. He wanted to find an area that did not have a party atmosphere; one that was not teeming with nightclubs. His search led him to Phuket's Karon Beach, a five kilometre stretch of white sand along the Andaman Sea. There were several resorts in the area that seemed to serve families rather than cater to singles and the night-club crowd. Reading through the reviews, and looking at the photos of the resorts, he found one that appealed to him. It was situated on a large beautifully landscaped acreage with hills on one side and ocean on the other. It looked peaceful. Even more appealing were the reviews.

"It's so bloody quiet," wrote English Bertie.

"It's like everyone goes to bed right after dinner," complained Funlovin' Fred.

"Great for Grandma, no nightlife, no swim-up bars, no fun," concluded Giselle99.

"All you can do here," GeorgieB grumbled, "is walk the beach or swim in one of the pools. BORING! BORING! BORING!"

Perfect, Justin thought. Absolutely perfect.

Justin emailed the manager to ask if he could get a reduced rate for a long-term stay since he planned to stay at least six weeks if not longer. The manager replied that the resort was fully booked until after the Christmas and New Year's holidays. If Justin could delay his visit until January, he would be pleased to offer him a significantly reduced rate, and to include access to the executive club lounge. Justin was pleased with this response. The timing couldn't be better. He reserved a room for eight weeks.

He then went to his travel agent to book the flight. His parents had offered to contribute to the cost of his flight, so he indulged himself by purchasing a business class ticket. This, he assumed, would provide a more peaceful and private journey. The travel agent described a variety of routings that were available. Justin booked a somewhat convoluted route through Singapore to Phuket. The flight would take longer than the more direct flights through Hong Kong but was much less expensive. He also hoped that the length of the trip would help put some psychological as well as physical distance between his life with Jennifer in Vancouver, and his future which remained unknown. With his passport, proof of a return ticket and sufficient funds in the bank, Justin then applied for and received a tourist visa from the Thai Consulate in downtown Vancouver. January will come, he told himself.

13

Ian and Fiona

Realizing that anyone, anywhere, at any time, could see the photos of her led Heather into a downward spiral of self-destructive behaviour. Without thinking about where she was going or what she was doing, she walked in downtown Halifax until she got tired and hungry. She was sitting in a doorway when a woman approached her.

"Hey, you look like you could use a friend," she said, "I'm Kayla. Come, I'll buy you a burger and we'll chat."

Heather told Kayla her story, tears welling in her eyes. Kayla expressed sympathy and offered Heather a place to sleep that night.

"And you know what," she added, "I am driving to Toronto tomorrow. You could come with me. I'd love to have you along. We don't need to tell your folks until after we are there and settled. I will make sure that you are okay."

Heather, confused and frightened, readily agreed.

Once in Toronto, things changed. There was no more talk of letting Ian and Fiona know where she was. There was little concern about Heather's wellbeing. Providing her with little more than space to sleep and basic food, Kayla introduced Heather to alcohol and drugs.

"They help get you through the day," she told Heather, "and they are harmless."

Once she determined that Heather had become dependent on the drugs, Kayla told her she needed to get a job to help pay for costs.

"What sort of job could I get?" Heather asked. "I'm too young, I should be in school."

"You can work for a friend of mine," Heather explained. "He's always looking for pretty girls to work for him." Within weeks, Heather had escaped the pimp and was living on the streets in a different part of Toronto. She survived the only way she knew how: by exchanging sexual activity for drugs, food, money, or shelter.

* * *

Unable to find Heather anywhere in the Halifax region, Ian and Fiona contacted police forces in every major city across the country. They pleaded for her return in the media, and they offered a reward for information that would lead to her. Ian begged God to bring the child back to them. But they could not find her.

The call they feared most finally came. A girl's body was found in a public washroom in a suburban Toronto mall. The Toronto police identified her after searching though missing persons' reports. They informed Ian and Fiona. Heather had just turned fifteen when she overdosed on OxyContin.

Ian and Fiona blamed themselves for having failed to protect Heather. Ian was left questioning his faith and feeling angry at a God who could allow a child to be hurt so horribly.

Fiona felt incompetent. How could she help the abused and neglected children in her caseload when she had so terribly failed with Heather, she wondered. Neither could continue with their employment. After ten days of abject despair, they each asked for and were granted a leave of absence from work. It was all they could do to look after the basic needs of the other children.

Ian and Fiona did little other than sit around mourning. This was not helping anyone. They were not feeling any better. The children were misbehaving at home due to the lack of attention from their parents. Maggie reverted to wetting her pants and crying at bedtime. Lachlan and Caitlin were also acting out at school. It was not until the principal at Lachlan's school, Marcie Mackenzie, came to visit and explained how Lachlan was being affected, that Fiona realized that something had to change. Somehow, they had to move on.

"You folks have had to deal with the most difficult of situations, we all understand that." Marcie had told them. "But I'm going to speak frankly here. You can't let it continue to paralyze you. You have three wonderful children who need you. They are hurt and confused. Lachlan asked me if it was his fault that Heather ran away. He thought maybe he had not been friendly enough. You don't want him believing that, do you? To help Lachlan, Caitlin, and Maggie you need to get yourselves together. You're no use like this."

Ian sighed. "You're right of course, but what can we do. We can't just take off."

"Actually," said Marcie with a broad smile on her face, "you can, and you will."

"I don't understand." Fiona looked quizzically at Marcie.

"It's like this," Marcie explained. "Your friends and your flock have been very worried about you. They met, brainstormed, and came to the conclusion that you need a real getaway. So, they raised enough money for the two of you to take a month off—."

"What would we do with a month off?" Fiona interrupted.

"You will be spending it in Thailand. Mrs. Smith, as you know. is a travel agent. She has recommended a resort at Karon Beach in Thailand that has a reputatlin for being relaxing and restorative."

Ian and Fiona sat in stunned silence.

"And before you ask," Marcie continued, "your sister Erin, Ian, has agreed to take care of the children during your absence. We Maritimers look after each other. It's all set."

She opened her bag and removed a large envelope which she handed to Ian. "Here's your booking. All the details of your flights and stay and tickets are here. Enjoy." She left.

Ian and Fiona were stunned. Neither had ever left Nova Scotia before. The thought of travelling to a country in Asia was terrifying. It was also exciting and energizing. They couldn't imagine leaving the children for a month, but the children adored their aunt Erin, and she was completely reliable.

"Would you guys be okay if we went away for a bit and Aunt Erin looked after you? They asked Caitlin and Lachlan.

"Can we still go to school" asked Lachlan.

"Will we be allowed to play with Benji?" Caitlin and Maggie both loved Erin's golden retriever.

It quickly became clear that the children were fine with the arrangement, so Ian and Fiona turned their attention to the details of the trip. They spent hours discussing the proposed trip; they wondered about the number of airline changes that would be needed, the facilities at the resort, and the safety of the country. It would all be so different from what they were used to.

Their holidays had been limited to taking the children to the local beaches and campgrounds. All three children loved camping. They enjoyed going to Porter's Lake which was less than an hour from their home and close to Lawrencetown Beach. They couldn't swim at Lawrencetown, as the water was too cold and too rough. But it was the perfect beach for walking and exploring, and there was a children's pool at the campsite. Other than the camping holidays, they had driven to Cape Breton to visit family. Thailand would be quite the adventure. Step one would be getting passports.

As they prepared for bed that night, Ian turned to Fiona.

"Do you realize that we have gone for hours thinking about something other than Heather? Not that we will, or should, ever forget her. But I think Marcie and our friends were right. Even talking about going away is helpful."

"Of course, we will never forget her. But yes, they are right. If we are to be good parents to those three wonderful kids of ours, and still be able to look after other foster children in the future, we need to recover."

Ian put his arms around Fiona and held her tightly. "We're starting that now," he said, kissing her deeply for the first time since Heather left.

14

Nigel

Nigel Smythe II stood at the conservatory window looking out over the manicured lawn. Behind it, through the tennis courts and the rose garden, he could see the river Thames meandering down toward Reading. It was a glorious spring day. It was, Nigel thought, a Robert Browning *Oh to be in England* sort of day. Nigel didn't feel particularly happy to be in England, but he didn't feel like travelling either. Turning his attention from the river to the grass, he noticed something grey and white at the edge of the lawn. Surely the gardener would not have left weeds or leaves behind, he thought. Finding his binoculars under the morning newspaper, Nigel focused in on the unknown object. Surprised at what he saw, he pulled on a sweater and loafers, and walked down to where the object lay. It was, as he had thought, a hedgehog. And if he was not mistaken, it was a hedgehog in trouble.

Due to his son's passion, Nigel knew more than many about hedgehogs. From infancy on, Harrison could not sleep without Spike his stuffed hedgehog, and before he settled down each night, he insisted on at least one reading of each of his favourite books, *Hedgies Surprise* and *The Very Helpful*

Hedgehog. And, being a typical child, Harrison asked endless questions about hedgehogs.

"Do hedgehogs like tummy rubs? Can hedgehogs swim? Do hedgehogs like biscuits? Why are they called hedgehogs, daddy, do they live in hedges?" And when he was learning to count, Harrison asked: "Can I count the spikes now?"

"Can you count to 6000?" Nigel had asked him.

Nigel's initial hunch was right. Not only was the hedgehog out late morning, itself a sign of trouble, but also, as he got close to it, Nigel could see that it had a damaged hind leg. He hoped it wasn't Wobbly Hedgehog Syndrome; that would be a death sentence. After getting a blanket from the shed to cover the hedgehog, Nigel called his friend Quentin.

Quentin was a vet who worked part-time at the Hedgehog Hospital at the Shepreth Wildlife Conservatory. It had been a busy year for the hospital with over eight hundred admissions, but Quentin said he had just finished a call and was in the area so he would stop by soon and check out the injured hedgie. Quentin added that he'd been meaning to drop by and see how Nigel was doing anyway. Nigel was relieved Quentin would be there soon.

Nigel could do no more for Harrison, but with Quentin's help, perhaps he could save this hedgehog. Waiting for Quentin, Nigel reflected on how much Harrison had enjoyed outings to the Hedgehog Hospital. Enough, he said to himself, as he realized he was sinking into unhappy memories.

Nigel walked to his study, sat at his computer, and brought up the manuscript he had started two years ago. He wondered if he would ever get it finished. He had experienced no difficulty getting a publisher from his initial proposal, but he was well behind the expected finish date. The publisher had already given him two extensions. He would not get another. On days when he worked on it, the project gave him the structure and meaning he lacked without Harrison. But he found it hard to focus on writing.

His goal was to complete a comprehensive book on the social construction of sexuality. He had finished the section on changing attitudes toward homosexuality. He had paid particular attention to the gross indecency law that came into effect in 1885. It was the law under which Oscar Wilde had been convicted in 1895, and Alan Turing in 1952. The fact that Turing was not pardoned until 2013, posthumously, appalled him. Nigel was grateful to have born in 1970, a mere three years after the law was taken off the books. It seemed so unfair, he thought, that where you were born, and when you were born, could make the difference between living your sexuality and being locked up for it.

His next section was going to be on cultural and historical changes in attitudes toward pederasty. His interest here stemmed from the experiences of a neighbour. Eighty-one-year-old Mr. Lawson had recently been incarcerated for a sexual relationship he'd had some sixty years earlier. Lawson had been twenty and the boy almost fifteen when the relationship started. Lawson's lawyer had described it as a consensual relationship. For six months, he told the court, they had enjoyed being together, and the decision to end the relationship was mutual. Lawson explained that he and the boy had stayed friends over the next decade. He even produced correspondence between them that he had kept. It supported his contention that there had been no coercion or hard feelings.

Nigel had been stunned when his Mr. Lawson was arrested, and the details of his crime were in the local paper. He had known him only as a married man, a father, and grandfather: as a man who was a well-respected member of the community. Was it possible that he had corrupted a minor as the press described? Why would he have had a sexual relationship with a young boy anyway? Was it possible that it was consensual? Had the boy been old enough to give informed consent? At what age, Nigel questioned, could one be expected to give informed consent? Was fifteen too young? Should there be a statute of limitations on all inappropriate sexual behaviours, he wondered, or just those involving violence? Was there any point in incarcerating a man in his eighties for behaviour that occurred once and so long ago? Nigel was confused. He hoped if he researched pederasty, he would be able to understand his neighbour's behaviour and the victim's response.

Nigel's initial research indicated that pederasty was legally and culturally sanctioned in some areas, but in Western countries was seen as abhorrent and confused with pedophilia. This didn't help. His editor had suggested he remove that section and focus on aspects of sexuality more socially acceptable to modern readers, such as cross dressing, gay marriage, and transgender youth. He initially had rejected his editor's suggestion but was now thinking maybe it was a good idea. He stared at the manuscript for fifteen minutes, then closed the file.

He walked back to the great room. Scanning his large array of CDs, Nigel selected a recording of Puccini's *Tosca*. The music would sooth him. The melodramatic story made Nigel's life seem less tragic than it felt when he looked back on it. As Placido Domingo started singing "E lucevan le stella," Nigel's favourite aria from *Tosca*, Nigel sat back and let the sublime music envelop him. The discordant chime of the doorbell startled him. Quentin had arrived. It was time to rescue the hedgehog. Leaving Domingo to sing about his impending death, Nigel went to the door.

15

Justin

The morning of his trip, Justin woke to a rare sight. Snow blanketed his Kitsilano neighbourhood. He realized immediately that it would take much longer than the usual half hour to get to the airport. He had prepared everything the night before, so right away he called for a cab. To his relief, the cab arrived quickly. But ten minutes later, Justin was so tense he felt on the verge of an explosion. The roads had not been plowed, and traffic was stop and go. Mostly stop.

Trying to control himself, Justin started some deep breathing exercises he had learned doing yoga. Deep breath in, blow it out slowly, deep breath in, blow it out slowly. It helped. They eventually arrived safely at the airport; the trip had taken over two hours.

Justin ran to the business class check-in desk. He was pleased to see only one person in front of him, but the pleasure did not last. First, it was a full fifteen minutes before the agent was free. Then, things got worse.

"Your flight to San Francisco has been cancelled sir."

"Did you re-book me? I have a connection to Singapore."

"Well, no sir, since you are travelling on points."

Justin had difficulty controlling himself.

"I paid full business fare for this flight," he managed to get out without screaming.

"Sir, you will have to join the re-booking line over there." The agent pointed to a long line of anxious looking would-be travellers. "The agent there will find you an alternate."

Seething, Justin went to the back of the line and phoned his travel agent. Ari was sympathetic and checked flights. There was a partner flight to Frisco, he told Justin, that would still allow him to make his connection. Hearing this, Justin went back to the agent he had been talking with and asked him to book him on that flight.

"Sorry sir," the agent replied, "we have just filled that flight. Maybe you should consider coming back tomorrow and trying then."

"Please call your supervisor."

Four hours passed while Justin talked to desk agents, supervisors, and airline executives. None could help. Exhausted and feeling desperate, he called the airport hotel. Maybe, he thought, it would be better just to stay over, get some sleep and leave in the morning. Having made that decision, he relaxed—until his call was answered.

"Yes sir," the reservation clerk said. "We do happen to have a room for tonight."

"That's so good to hear," said Justin, pulling out his charge card.

"It's a lovely room, sir."

"I better just check the cost before I book it," Justin said, thinking that even if it was a few hundred dollars, to lie on a clean bed in a warm room and get some sleep would be worth it.

"Tonight's rate sir is twelve hundred."

"Sorry, I'm not sure I heard you. The room is how much for one night?"

"Twelve hundred dollars. sir."

Justin felt his body flush with a mixture of rage and frustration. He managed to turn off his phone and get it back into his pocket without dropping it or screaming expletives aloud. He then walked back to the desk agent. This could not get worse, Justin thought to himself, prematurely as it turned out. The agent was clearing his desk.

"Sir, it is time for my break. I suggest you either go home and try another day or see if your travel agent can find you anything. Goodbye."

Justin stood speechless and wondered if the steam he felt coming out of his eyes and ears was visible. He called Ari.

Five and a half hours after arriving at the airport, Justin had an itinerary thanks to the extensive efforts of Ari. The route was considerably less than desirable. Vancouver to Seattle and on to San Francisco in economy with no compensation for having already paid for business. He then had a three-hour wait, an overnight flight to Hong Kong, another long wait, a flight to Singapore, another long wait, and then a flight to Phuket. But at least he would be on his way. He emailed the resort to alert them to the change in his arrival time.

Fifty-five hours after leaving his home in Kitsilano, a drained Justin arrived in Phuket. On arrival, his luck changed.

His luggage was on the carousel, and the car he had pre-arranged was waiting for him. The driver greeted him with a bottle of ice-cold water and a cold towel. This was a welcome treat after the long trip and the heat of his new surroundings. He loaded Justin's bags into the trunk, and they set off.

The drive to the resort was interesting enough that his tension began to dissipate. They passed through small towns where vendors sold supplies from roadside shacks, and along streets that were cluttered with more overhead wires than Justin would have thought possible. And seemingly the entire population was weaving in and out of traffic on motorbikes somehow just missing the Toyota in which he sat comfortably.

Ninety minutes after leaving the airport, they pulled into an oasis of calm and breathtaking natural beauty. Feeling like he could breathe again, Justin checked in. To his delight, the hotel had upgraded him to a corner room. There was a wrap-around balcony and floor to ceiling windows which over-looked the long sandy beach and the Andaman Sea. On the bed, 'Welcome' was spelled out in bougainvillea petals. On the desk was a bottle of wine chilling in an ice bucket. Beside it was a box of chocolates and a plate of fruit. He stared in amazement. Maybe, he thought, that awful journey was worth it. After reluctantly sweeping the petals off the bed cover, Justin fell onto the bed and slept soundly for twelve hours.

PART 2: THAILAND
January-March 2018

16

The Meet and Greet

Justin woke early to bird song and sunshine. Still feeling groggy from the long trip, he decided to take a walk on the beach before having breakfast. The vegetation was lush, and it seemed like every wall was hidden under frothy mounds of bougainvillea in neon shades of red, pink, and purple. The surrounding hills were deep green, and the sky a brilliant blue. Walking through the property, he began to feel more at peace than he had for a long time.

Between his room and the beach, Justin walked by two swimming pools and three ponds. Standing at the edge of one of the larger ponds were three storks. Their appearance enchanted Justin. He stopped, watching them for a few minutes. He then walked past the small pond that was outside the resort's spa. It was teeming with red, black, and white patterned koi. When he stopped to look at them, the koi swam up to the edge and looked expectantly at him. He realized they, like him, had not yet had breakfast. "Sorry guys," he said, as he walked on.

Arriving at the beach, Justin was surprised to see several people walking or jogging along the shore, despite the early hour. He noticed a few feral dogs playing in the ocean and chasing each other across the sand. They seemed to be having as much fun as children on the beach. Jenn would have loved this, he thought to himself. The ocean looked tempting, but Justin had noticed a jelly fish warning, so he restricted himself to walking barefoot at the edge of the water. He recalled being stung by a jelly fish three years ago while swimming in the Caribbean Ocean. He had experienced an allergic reaction to the sting and was in considerable pain from it. Since then, he preferred to do his swimming in pools.

Justin walked for about half an hour down the beach before feeling hungry. He turned around and headed back to the resort for breakfast. Looking up at the hills as he walked back, he noticed the Big Buddha at the top of the hill. It was an impressive sight, albeit, he thought, a bit odd. A few longtail boats were coming toward the shore; he assumed they would be offering rides to tourists later in the morning.

Back at the resort, Justin had breakfast at the outdoor restaurant. The buffet options were vast, and he thoroughly enjoyed a variety of fresh fruit, many of which he did not recognize, and a made-to-order vegetarian omelette. One glass of mango juice and three cups of coffee later, he was ready to finish unpacking his bags and then to relax by the pool with a book.

When he returned to his room, Justin found an invitation from the manager to a special cocktail party for guests staying a month or longer. It was to be held that evening at 6:30. Despite not feeling social, Justin decided to go. He was curious about what sort of people the other guests would be. He spent the morning by the pool, had a nap in the afternoon, and after a shower was ready to attend the party.

Seven guests, each staying at least four weeks, had gathered at sunset on the sand in an area bordered with small twinkling lights. A large table displayed a generous selection of wines and cocktails, and traditionally dressed servers offered trays of appetizers. The magical atmosphere was enhanced by three peacocks wandering around looking askance at the guests as though their space was being invaded. From the trees came the sound of a bird shouting what sounded to Justin as "surreal, surreal." Indeed it is, he thought as the manager approached and introduced himself to each guest.

Justin recognized an older couple who were standing by the table as people he had passed while walking the beach that morning.

"Oh, hi there, didn't we see you on the beach this morning?" Simon asked Justin.

"This is my husband Simon and I'm Alison. We're here from New York." Alison thrust her hand toward Justin.

"Justin Marley. I'm from Canada."

"Those two are from Canada also," Simon said, pointing to Fiona and Ian. "Maybe you know them? And that British dude is Lord Nigel something the second. Fancy. Haven't met the other guy yet, the one who is all elegantly dressed. Let's go and meet him."

Malcolm, who was also from New York, stood by the table. He looked quite striking. He was tall and thin, and impeccably dressed in beige chinos and a pale blue designer T-shirt. He wore a colourful bandana loosely knotted around his neck, and an earring sparkled from his right ear. Justin noticed Malcolm could not take his eyes off Nigel. The three of them chatted for a few minutes. Having said hello to everyone and thanked the manager, Justin left early. He was not ready for a long evening of socializing.

Malcolm and Nigel talked with the manager for a few moments before exchanging niceties with the Canadian couple, who they were learned were Ian and Fiona, and with Simon and Alison, the older Americans. The conversation centred on when each had arrived, where they lived, what they did for a living, and how long they were staying. Nigel expressed his particular interest in the peacocks. Simon, who could never stay out of professor mode for long, explained that as far as he knew, some cultures considered peacocks to be equivalent to gods, presumably because of their striking colours and tail feathers. He also noted that many Buddhists consider the peafowl to represent wisdom. Alison was relieved there were no apparent links to Trump, Hitler, or Nazis.

Nigel left the cocktail party feeling invigorated. He sat in his room, looking out at the eerie green lights of the fishing boats that dotted the horizon and thinking about the guests he had met. Justin from Canada seemed nice enough, he thought, and the two couples seemed friendly. But of most interest to him was Malcolm from New York. Nigel was attracted to Malcolm and he had a hunch his feelings were reciprocated. They had talked at length at the cocktail party about the location, the peacocks, the wine, and the snacks. Throughout the conversation, Malcolm had focused his attention on Nigel. His body language had been flirtatious.

Nigel had met and held Malcolm's gaze. They had agreed to meet the following evening at the bar.

Nigel spent the next day thinking about Malcolm and wondering if he was ready for a relationship. He told himself he was getting way ahead of reality and forced himself to calm down by having a long and vigorous morning swim. That afternoon he napped, then had another swim. He resolved to be cool when they met that evening.

They sat together in the outdoor bar, enjoying the Zen-like atmosphere, and the cooler evening air. They chatted over a few bottles of Singha, a local beer they found they both liked. The conversation stayed light. Neither discussed the circumstances that brought them to Thailand. It turned out that Malcolm not only shared Nigel's love of opera but also that he was a tenor whose goal in life was to sing at the Met. He would be happy with any role, he told Nigel, but his greatest desire was to play Rodolfo, the poet, in *La Boheme*, or Mario Cavaradossi, the painter, in *Tosca*. Nigel wondered if he was dreaming. Feeling like an infatuated teenager, he decided he'd met the love of his life. Slow down, he said to himself, you're both here for a month. But he could not contain his excitement. Before he blurted out something embarrassingly juvenile, the others who they had met last night wandered over and invited the pair to join them for a nightcap.

As the seven of them sat around the table, Simon chuckled and announced that he would think of the group as the MOE gang. "We are," he said, "quite as diverse as the characters in *Murder on the Orient Express*."

"And which of us," Nigel asked, "is M. Hercule Poirot? And," he added, "will there be a murder?"

17

Getting to Know Malcolm

"So, what did you guys do today?" Simon asked Ian. The group was gathered round a large table in the executive lounge. They were enjoying the happy hour drinks and snacks that were among the perks of the status upgrade they had all received. It had become a routine.

"Such a busy day," sighed Ian. "We walked the beach, read books by the pool, had a nap and here we are. I think Fiona and I are still getting used to the heat. It's not exactly like this in Halifax, even in the height of summer."

"I had the most wonderful morning," Nigel gushed. "I took the tour of the Phuket Elephant Sanctuary. My vet friend at home, Quentin, had told me about it and recommended it. I'm so glad I went. What an amazing place. It wasn't at all like the typical disrespectful tourist stuff where people ride on elephants, and hug their trunks, and generally disturb them. We just got to see them freely roaming and swimming, playing, and socializing all free of human touch or even noise. It was breathtaking. And oh my, the environment. The elephants live on thirty acres of the most beautiful rainforest I could have ever imagined. It was such a marvellous example of how rescued animals should be treated. How Harrison would have loved it."

"Who's Harrison?" Fiona and Alison asked in unison. Malcolm sat up.

"Harrison—er, did I mention Harrison? Some other time."

There was a moment of silence.

Sensing his discomfort and wishing to lessen the tension, Alison described her shopping trip into the town. She was excited, she said, to have found some inexpensive gorgeous silk kimonos at the market. She planned to go back and buy one for her daughter-in-law Amy, one for her granddaughter Zoe, and a few for her friends. As she talked, the others relaxed again. Ian went to get a plate of snacks for them to share, and all the drinks were filled. There was a brief lull in conversation. Looking out the window, Justin noticed the sun was starting its nightly descent into the Andaman Sea. The lounge was on the fifteenth floor of the building and overlooked the ocean. The view was always lovely, but at sunset it was breathtakingly beautiful. The sun, a bright scarlet perfect circle gradually sunk into the darkening ocean at the horizon. Justin got up and took a photo with his phone. Simon and Alison followed suit.

Once the sun had disappeared, they returned to their table. Justin, who did not want to talk about himself, took the opportunity to ask Malcolm how he had decided upon Phuket and how long he was staying.

Malcolm said, "I could ask the same question of all of you.

But sure, I'll go first. We're all here for a while." They all listened with interest.

Malcolm explained that as a child, he had come here with his parents for family vacations. His dad, who was an executive with an international software company, occasionally had business in Hong Kong. Sometimes Malcolm and his mom would go with him on the business trips and then the family would vacation in Phuket before returning to New York. He remembered the Phuket vacations fondly. All the staff were friendly, which had made his eight-year-old self feel grown up and important. He remembered the swimming pool with the long twisty slide that went through a cave and a waterfall. In his memories, it was Malcolm's happy place. This was his first trip back as an adult.

"What made you come back?" asked Ian, "if you don't mind me asking."

"I needed some time out."

Malcolm described to the group how burned out he had been feeling, and how unsure of his future. His father had insisted that Malcolm obtain an MBA in business. Malcolm regretted his compliance. His passion was music. But his daily life as a data analyst on Madison Avenue was far removed from the beauty of bel canto.

"You mean you are a number cruncher?" asked Simon.

"It's much more than that. I have to manipulate the data I dig up in ways that allow the manipulation of consumers. It's an awful way to make a living. I have to use my knowledge of computer language and statistics to identify new market needs, new product uses, and potential new groups of customers. I hate it, I hate every minute of it."

"I understand hating statistics," cut in Alison. "I still remember having to learn statistics during my Master's program. In those days, psych students were supposed to not only understand which statistical method to use in the different kinds of research, but also, we were expected to work the damn formulas out with a handheld calculator. Unbelievable! I was always hopeless at math; always hated it. I remember those days well. We were living in student housing and had no laundry facilities there. Twice a week I would have to go to the local laundromat. So, I used to take the stats text to the laundromat and place it open on the top of the dryer in the hope that some of the information would get absorbed by my jeans." She chuckled at the memory.

Malcolm smiled at her. "And how did that work for you?"

"Oh, really well," she answered grinning, "I just got more and more traumatized. There was this one day in class, the prof started talking about a tie, and I panicked and asked him to explain what he meant by a tie. He sneered at me and said, what do you think I am talking about Alison, a cravat? It was so embarrassing. The other students were in hysterics. But Malcolm, why haven't you quit?"

"That sounds so logical, but I'm not sure what else I could do now." Malcolm explained that at first, he had stuck it out because he did not want to disappoint his father. A couple of years ago his father had died, and soon afterward so did his mother. By then he was established in the job, and was not ready to start over or lose his comfortable apartment in the city. He had tried to compensate for hating the job by immersing himself in music at every opportunity. Saturdays he taught voice to children; he taught an opera appreciation class at a local college one evening a week, and he auditioned for and participated in as many concerts, recitals, musicals, and operas as he could.

"I loved teaching the children, and the opportunities to perform," he said, "but it was unsustainable. I reached the point of complete exhaustion and needed a break. I needed distance, time, and space, to figure out a more livable and meaningful future. So, I sublet my apartment and came here. I'm hoping it will be healing. So far, it looks great." He smiled at Nigel.

18

Good Times

The next evening, there was a special seafood buffet at the resort's outdoor restaurant. After a couple of drinks in the lounge, Simon suggested they all go to the buffet. The response from all was an enthusiastic yes. There seemed to be a tacit agreement that tonight the conversation would remain strictly superficial. Simon called the restaurant from the lounge and was assured that there was space for the group. When they arrived, some thirty minutes later, a large table, beside the pool and close to the palm fringed edge of the restaurant, was ready for them. They each had a glass of wine, enjoying the view, the warmth of the evening sun, and the gentle breezes. But they did not wait long before eating. The aromas were tantalizing and rendered them salivating like Pavlov's dogs.

There were grilled lobsters and prawns, some kind of stuffed baked white fish none of them recognized, steamed mussels, oysters Rockefeller, grilled octopus, and calamari, along with a wide array of salads, rice, potatoes, roasted vegetables, and breads. The dessert table was laden with fruit, puddings, cakes, and ice creams. It was easy to restrict the conversation to the food. They all left happy and sated. Before going their separate ways for the night, they agreed to go for dinner as a group once a week. Simon let them know it was Alison's birthday the next week. They agreed that would be an occasion for a special dinner. Simon had heard about a restaurant nearby that was perched on the edge of a cliff overlooking the ocean and was reputed to have superb authentic Thai dishes. He made the reservation.

In between these special dinners, Justin enjoyed solitude. He liked the weekly dinners and the regular evening socializing but treasured solo activities during the day. He got up early in the mornings to attend yoga classes and spent some time each day meditating. In between these activities he spent hours walking the beach, swimming in the pool, and reading books on Buddhism. It was a routine he found therapeutic. He realized he was gradually thinking more about the good times with Jennifer than her tragic end, and he was moving from a focus on what he had lost to what he had enjoyed. He was feeling better.

One evening, thinking about his students and their interest in transgender issues, he decided to go to the Simon Cabaret which was just outside Phuket. He had heard about the ladyboys and their Vegas style show. This would be in stark contrast to his love of peace and all things Buddhist, but it might be good for him, he decided, to step out of his comfort zone.

The show started out pretty much as he had expected. As advertised, Justin saw the ladyboys had very feminine features; they were slim, pretty, and had great body proportions. Wearing flamboyant costumes and elaborate makeup, they danced and lip-synced with incredible skill. Justin was relaxed and enjoying the show from his prime front row seat when the spotlight fell on him. Before he could figure out what was happening, a generously proportioned dancer was leaning over him, rubbing his face between her massive breasts, fake he assumed, and leaving big red lipstick kisses on his forehead. He sat frozen with embarrassment. Feeling immensely self-conscious, he quietly thanked God that no one he knew was there. At least, he thought, you were not allowed to take photos during the show. This would live on only in his memory. He was relieved when the show ended. He found a washroom and scrubbed his forehead clean before finding a tuk-tuk to take him back to the resort. He decided his next trip would be to the Chalong Temple. There was, he decided, something to be said for staying in one's comfort zone.

Malcolm and Nigel spent some time together each day but, beyond brief hello and goodnight kisses, they did not advance their friendship to a more intimate level. It was too early for that. Although Nigel had been comfortable with casual sex for some time, he was nervous about getting physical too soon with someone he hoped to have a serious and long-term relationship with. But they did enjoy going for walks together, and some days sat beside each other at the pool reading. Malcolm was reading Joseph Volpe's book about the Met opera, *The Toughest Show on Earth*, and Nigel was reading books he had picked up at the airport in Hong Kong on the flora and fauna of Thailand. He identified some of the wildlife he had seen at the elephant sanctuary but remained most fascinated with the semi-tame peacocks that, he realized, liked to wander around the pool. One afternoon, he was dozing off in his lounger when a peacock walked right up to him and made its signature loud honking noise. It was a memorable moment. Malcolm managed to capture the startled expression on Nigel's face, and the peacock's stare in a priceless photo. It provided a great deal of amusement at the lounge that evening.

The following evening, Nigel and Malcolm went to the Cabaret. They were intrigued by Justin's description of it, although Justin had left out his unwitting involvement in the entertainment. Nigel thought he might be able to get some information for his book on sexuality, and maybe even a photo of one of the ladyboys to include. Justin had told him that photos were not allowed during the show, but for some reasonable number of Baht or US dollars, the ladyboys were happy to pose outside after the show.

Simon and Alison, and Fiona and the Rev, as the gang called Ian, became friends and enjoyed spending time together. Fiona and Alison went on a few shopping trips. Alison wanted to buy some additional souvenirs for Michael and Amy and their children, Zach and Zoe, who were both teenagers. She already had a T-shirt for Zach and the kimono for Zoe. Fiona was eager to find some souvenirs of Thailand for Lachlan, Caitlin, and Maggie. She missed them more than she would have thought possible. Despite the time difference, Fiona and Ian were able to talk with the children by Skype most days and knew that they each were hoping for some toys or books that would be what Thai children played with. The two couples also went together on a few day trips to local sites.

The trip they enjoyed most was the Early Bird tour of the Phi Phi Islands. None had snorkelled before, and they all found the experience exhilarating. The highlight of the trip for each of them was seeing the monkeys on the appropriately named Monkey Beach. The lush vegetation on the cliff was home to the crab-eating, tree-leaping, Long-Tailed Macaques. Alison was tempted to try and get close to one of the monkeys, but Simon intervened.

"Remember what our tour guide said, Alison. These guys look really cure, but they can be extremely aggressive. There's probably good reason why he told us not to get close to them or feed them."

They were less satisfied with their so-called cultural tour. Parts of it were okay. Seeing the Big Buddha up close was more interesting that they had anticipated and made them realize why it was so revered. It was hard to tell from the beach how magnificent the 150-foot marble sculpture was. The history of the area relayed by the tour driver was of interest also, but they did not appreciate the stops at souvenir shops and jewellery factories. Fiona and Alison had already done their shopping at local bazaars that sold authentic Thai souvenirs. The shopping stops on this tour were oriented toward undiscerning tourists who happily purchased mass produced items rather than the exquisite, handcrafted signature products of Thailand: fabrics, triangle cushions, wicker baskets, pottery dishes, lacquerware, and wooden carvings.

* * *

Most evenings, the MOE gang exchanged stories about

their day's experiences over drinks in the lounge. The nightly sunset show, as they had begun to think of it, was a wonderful accompaniment to the drinks and chat. Malcolm said it reminded him of when he was in Cairns some years ago. Each night there, he would watch what he called the bat show. The bats spent their days, he told them, hanging upside down of course, in trees outside the library, and at sundown they would fly off to forage. The sky would be almost black with them. He much preferred the sunset, he commented. The routine of these happy hours became more enjoyable as they felt increasingly connected with each other, and integral parts of each other's daily lives. None anticipated the events that this cohesion and comfort precipitated.

19

Nigel Tells his Story

After a few weeks had passed getting to know each other and the local area, Simon could no longer quell his curiosity. During the sunset show, at the end of a day where no one had gone anywhere, he asked Nigel if he was okay. Nigel nodded.

"Nigel, a while ago you mentioned a Harrison. Are you ready to tell us who he is?"

"You know Nigel," Alison added, "I get the feeling something has been bothering you and maybe you need to talk about it. We are here to listen if that's so."

Nigel put his drink down, looked uncomfortable, but then took a deep breath and replied.

"You are right Alison. Maybe I should talk about it; it's going to be hard, and I shall probably get emotional and embarrassed, but I'll try. Maybe we should all fill our glasses first."

They did, and sat back down, gathered closer around him.

Nigel took another deep breath. "I loved Harrison more than anyone; I would have died for him."

Malcolm fidgeted.

"He was my son, my beautiful, intelligent, kind and wonderful son."

Malcolm looked both relieved and concerned.

"I should add that I was married. It didn't work out." He paused for a moment before adding, "I guess none of you is surprised to hear that." He took a sip of wine before continuing.

"When Harrison was five, he was diagnosed as having a peanut allergy. His doctor decided to monitor him, and to start a course of oral immunotherapy if there was any indication that the allergy would become life-threatening. It was not that this would cure the allergy, but it would reduce the likelihood of him suffering a severe reaction. I was terrified," Nigel continued, "that he would go into anaphylactic shock. And very relieved when the doctor decided not to go through with the immunotherapy."

Nigel went on to explain that he made sure that he, Harrison, and Harrison's teachers all kept an epinephrine autoinjector with them because there were so many foods that contained peanuts. Even some chocolates and ice creams that you wouldn't expect to have any traces of nuts, he explained, often had traces of peanuts. He also made sure that Harrison was always wearing a medical alert bracelet.

"I thought I had him protected," Nigel sighed, "but as it turned out it wasn't enough."

Nigel stopped and took a drink; the others waited, saying nothing. He continued.

"When Harrison was twelve, the doctors recommended that he have a tonsillectomy. Since starting school, he had suffered a lot of bad throat infections including a couple of times when the infection seemed to be bacterial, and antibiotics didn't help. I remember one year, he had six different throat infections. Anyway, I checked with the doctors, and I read some medical info, and it seemed like because Harrison did not have any other medical issues, other than the peanut allergy, the risks from the surgery were extremely low. And there was a good possibility that the surgery would mean no more of the endless infections. So, I agreed. It is a decision that haunts me to this day, the worst decision of my life. If only...." His voice wavered and weakened.

Malcolm, who was sitting next to him, reached over and slowly rubbed Nigel's back.

"Do you want to continue," Fiona asked, "or call it a night?"

"No," Nigel replied, "having got this far, I will tell you the rest of the story."

As all listened intently, he described what happened.

Nigel explained how he had wanted Harrison's surgery to be done at the Great Ormond Street Hospital because it had such a great reputation. But Harrison's doctor had convinced him otherwise.

"Lord Smythe," the doctor told me, "you know we don't do as many tonsillectomies as we used to. But it remains a routine, low-risk procedure especially for children your son's age. Any local hospital can easily do it. There's no need to go to Ormond Street. Your boy will be fine, and anyway we'll only be keeping him in overnight."

"So, after he said that, I reminded him of Harrison's allergy. Given that, wouldn't he be safer at Ormond Street rather than our local hospital. The doctor assured me that the allergy would be on Harrison's chart and anyway, he had joked trying to calm my fears, we don't usually give nuts to kids who've had their tonsils out. Just ice cream and the like."

"I got quite agitated when he said this. Surely a doctor would know that ice cream can have peanuts in it. I pointed this out. He patted my shoulder and promised that Harrison's allergy would be considered before he was given anything to eat or drink, and that they would be extra careful not to give him ice cream that had any nuts or could have been contaminated by nuts. I guess I believed him," Nigel concluded.

After another brief pause, Nigel continued to describe what happened. The day of the surgery came. Harrison brought Spike, his oldest and still favourite toy, out and asked if he thought others would laugh at him taking a ratty old stuffed animal with him. Spike went to the hospital. As the doctor had said, the surgery went well. Harrison woke up a bit groggy and sore, but feeling okay, and wanting to watch his favourite nature show on TV. Nigel was vastly relieved everything was over, so he put the show on the TV that was attached to the end of Harrison's bed, and left to go home for a few hours, promising to be back in the evening. When he returned two hours later, Harrison was dead.

"Oh my God," Alison blurted out. "What happened? I never heard of a kid dying from a tonsillectomy."

Nigel continued. Unable to resuscitate him when he was found, the nurses checked everything that may have led to his death. The only thing they noticed was a bowl on the bedside table that looked like it had been full of ice cream. Later analysis showed that the ice cream had contained traces of peanuts. The hospital team concluded that Harrison had suffered anaphylaxis from eating the ice cream. But where did the ice cream come from? They had no idea. He was not due for any food, and his allergy was clearly marked on his chart. There had been a food cart in the area for other patients, but nothing for Harrison other than a glass of apple juice. They figured out that Harrison must have seen the ice cream on the cart and taken it to sooth his throat.

"I didn't buy it," Nigel said. "He knew never to eat anything unless he was sure what was in it, and he had been told many times about ice cream. He was not a stupid kid, and he was not a disobedient one. But now he was a dead one."

Malcolm moved closer and put his arm over Nigel's shoulders. On his other side, Fiona placed her hand on his arm. They were all shocked. Alison was crying. Ian was praying.

"Did you get a lawyer, did you sue?"

"No Simon, I was too upset to do anything until much later. It took almost a year before I could bring myself to do anything other than occasionally get out of bed. Then I hired a private detective. It's still hard to believe what he discovered. A sixteen-year-old girl, Miranda Jones, was helping with hospital meal deliveries as part of her community service sentence. She had been convicted of stealing Rohypnol for her boyfriend who would then rape girls while Miranda filmed them; then they'd threaten to post the film unless the girl gave them money. Horrendous but true."

Ian and Fiona paled and clasped hands.

"On the record, this was a first offence, but, get this, my detective discovered that an infant she had been babysitting some years back had died in her care. It was assumed SIDs, but he thinks it likely she smothered the baby. Then a year later, her younger sibling drowned while she was in charge. Another terrible accident, or who knows. Seemed to me that she was one very disturbed and dangerous kid. Anyway, she was at the hospital that day, and she had the food cart. George, the detective, found a witness who said he heard her take the ice cream into Harrison and say, 'here you might like this.' 'Is it peanut free,' my son had asked, trusting her. 'Oh, sure,' she'd replied, 'guaranteed, I checked'."

As far as George could figure, Miranda had taken the ice cream off the tray to make the tray easier to carry and then forgotten about it. It was at the end of her shift and she wanted to get going to meet her boyfriend, so she gave it to the nearest patient. It seems that she didn't intend to kill Harrison; she just didn't care. Her negligence caused his death. I took the evidence to the police, but they weren't interested. The case was closed. Anyway, it was too late to do anything by then and of course nothing I could do would bring back my Harrison."

20

Introducing Criss-Cross

After Nigel's story, it was a restless night. Nigel felt a profound sadness after talking about Harrison, and the others reflected on their own losses. The next morning, in harmony with their moods, the weather had changed. Instead of the usual brilliant sunshine, the sky was a mass of dark, angry, foreboding clouds. By mid-morning, the wind was howling between the buildings, and the tropical rains were pelting down. The rain did not last, but the sky remained cloudy and the humidity levels high.

Coming into the lounge for happy hour that evening, Justin commented, "The night was 'ot and 'umid." Simon got the reference immediately and laughed.

"Danny DeVito and Billy Crystal, *Throw Momma From the Train*. Did you guys see that movie?"

All had except for the Rev and Fiona. But Fiona said she had read the book *Strangers on a Train*, by Patricia Highsmith, on which the movie was based.

"Criss-cross," laughed Alison. "You kill mine and I'll kill yours. Maybe one of us should take care of Miranda? Not that we would of course, this is real life, not a novel or a movie. But we can fantasize. What do you think Nigel? Wouldn't you like to see the end of Miranda?"

She looked around the table. "Okay, who'll volunteer to off Miranda? And who would you like Nigel to take care for you."

"Geez Alison," Simon said looking at her askance, "I've never heard you sound like a gangster before. But what of it, Lord Nigel? Would you do criss-cross?"

Nigel looked uncomfortable. He avoided answering the question. "I guess we will not see the sunset tonight," he commented trying to change the subject. It didn't work.

Justin, who had started happy hour rather early in the rainy afternoon said, "Well I don't know about the rest of you, but I have someone I'd sure like to see dead." And he told them about Jennifer and her uncle, and how his abuse of her had led to her death.

"I did some research later. Did you know that suicide in adulthood is often the result of childhood sexual abuse? In fact, I read that kids who are sexually abused are three times more likely to commit suicide later than others. And things that most people would just get upset or depressed about can lead to suicide. That's what happened to my Jennifer. She had a really bad day. Other people having a really bad day would come home and vent, or drink, or kick the dog or something. Not kill themselves. But even so, even though I know that it was her uncle who caused her death," he added, "even though he ruined my life, I don't think I could arrange for his murder. I really believe that killing is always wrong." Embarrassed by the tears in his eyes, Justin got up and went to refill his wine glass. The others followed.

Back at the table, Fiona announced that she and Ian had a horribly similar story.

"What an incredible coincidence. I can't believe this. It was sexual abuse that led to the death of a child we were fostering and wanted to adopt. Her biological mother allowed her boyfriend, who she knew damn well was a pedophile and sexual predator, to groom Heather, take nude photos of her, and post them online. The social workers insisted Heather visit her mother; they had no idea Alexander, the pedophile boyfriend, was in the picture. The poor child never told us. She fussed a lot about the visits, but we never knew why, although we realized something was upsetting her. The social worker just dismissed our concerns. The bastard posted almost nude photos of Heather online for all the kids at school, and I guess people anywhere with computer access, to see. She was bullied mercilessly, ran away, and before we could find her, she had died on the streets of Toronto."

Ian added, "I'd sure like to see those two get what they deserve."

"There've been cases where I lived," added Justin. "Kids who've had a history of family abuse or neglect are super vulnerable to pedophiles. We had a girl at our school who got involved with a guy on a chat room. She thought she was being friends with a boy her age. The jerk won her trust, and then got her involved in sex acts which he taped and distributed. She didn't suicide, but had terrible panic disorder, anxiety, and depression. She had to drop out of school. Last I heard she was in a mental health facility."

"What's with these guys?" asked the Rev. "I don't understand how they can knowingly destroy girls' lives. I suspect it's more widespread than we know."

"This is incredible," Alison said sounding quite heated. "I can't believe we all seem to have suffered an incredibly tragic loss caused by a selfish, evil, fucked-up person."

"All?" asked Justin.

"Not me." Malcolm said.

"We lost our beautiful daughter, Melody, to a bitch drunk driver who has never been held accountable because of her family connections. That was some years ago now, but how I would love to have my revenge or her, especially since I am quite sure she has caused the death of others since. She's an awful apology of a human being."

"My God, I wonder if that's why we have connected with each other. It's rather eerie. Is that why you came here, to recover from a loss?" Simon asked Fiona. Fiona nodded.

Nigel spoke up. "I came to recover from the loss of Harrison. After I found out about Miranda, I was even more angry and disturbed about his death. I became increasingly paralyzed. I stayed awake all night and went around like a zombie all day. I was working on a book, but I just couldn't concentrate. My friends urged me to do something, to get right away, or to go to some sort of residential retreat. My friend Quentin had heard about Phuket so he looked up some places and thought maybe here would be good for me. Being in nature has always calmed me down, Quentin knew that. I think he was right. I started to feel better as soon as I got here. There's something about all the trees, the flowers, and the ocean that's very restorative."

"I agree with you, Nigel," said Justin. "I wanted to learn more about Buddhism, plus I have relatives in Bangkok who I have never met. I thought it would help me to meet them, and I'm finding the yoga and meditation exercises to be very helpful. Seems like we are all here to forget and to heal, not to plan murders."

"True," Simon responded, "but, maybe it's cathartic thinking about it."

"And maybe even more so planning it," Alison added.

21

Just Joking

The following morning, the sun reappeared and moods lightened. Simon and Alison went for a long walk in the morning, did a little shopping, and spent the afternoon reading by the pool. Fiona and Ian walked the beach for about two hours while discussing the conversation of the previous evening. They were struck by the shared tragedies and tried to find some meaning in them. Justin spent almost the entire day in meditation and yoga. He found it a good antidote to the tense evening they had spent. Malcolm and Nigel sat together in a quiet shaded area of the resort and talked about their plans for the future. Although neither explicitly stated it, there seemed to be an understanding between them that they would spend their futures together.

That evening the gang was going out again for their weekly special dinner. Feeling more relaxed and more cohesive after their happy hour drinks, the gang walked into town to a local traditional restaurant, to enjoy an outdoor meal together. The evening air was clear and warm, the sunset show was back on, and they all studiously avoided talking about their losses. As they walked along, they were surprised at how lively and busy the streets and markets were. Vendors standing at colourful busy stalls were selling clothing, soaps, spices, Pad Thai, and fresh fish. The lush colours, rich odours, and crowd noise seemed exotic, and somehow reassured them that all was well with the world.

At the restaurant they ordered a Singha beer each for before dinner, and wine to have with the meal. They were drinking more than usual. Ian realized this, but decided it was in response to the revelations of the previous evening and decided not to comment. By the time the food came, he did note that they seemed to be well-oiled. Ian and Fiona were feeling the effects more than the others, since they rarely drank alcohol at home, but they also continued drinking. By the second bottle of wine, all inhibitions were lost, and Alison returned to the previous evening's suggestion that they could, like Highsmith's characters, get away with murder if they hit each other's targets.

Simon and Alison started by volunteering to kill Miranda for Nigel. It would be easy, they said. They explained that their son Michael had moved to London with his wife Amy, soon after they both graduated. The couple had no trouble getting work visas which allowed them to stay up to five years. They hadn't planned on staying longer, but both ended up with jobs they loved. Michael was working at the US Embassy, and Amy had a part-time job teaching English Literature at a private girls' high school. They had thought that they would leave London once they had children, but time passed, and they did not move. Once the children started school, Michael and Amy realized they were there for good. They liked that children started school much earlier than in the United States.

Reception, as they called the first year, began when the kids were four. Michael also was convinced that the school system was much better than that in the US. They applied for, and received, immigration status.

"We need to get over there. We haven't seen our grandkids for two years," explained Alison. "Two years ago, they all came to New York, we had a great time. But two years is a long time at their ages. They were still kids, now Zoe is fifteen and Zach is thirteen—teenagers. And we have to give them all the souvenir stuff we bought for them. So, you see, we have good reason to be in London. And who would ever suspect us, a couple of old professors, of murdering an English girl while visiting our grandkids. Easy! You just need to tell us where she is, and what she looks like. We'll figure out the rest."

Assuming they were joking, and having now had three drinks, Ian decided to play the game.

"Hey, we have been meaning to go to the Vancouver area, and maybe up into northern British Columbia to see some relatives who live there, so we could do that and then we could take care of that horrible uncle you talked about, Justin." Ian added smiling.

"Are you serious Rev?" Justin looked surprised.

"Sure, why not. You know, as it says in *Leviticus* chapter 24, versus 17 through 21, an eye for and eye, a tooth for a tooth. Just as another person has received injury from him, so it will be given to him." Ian, uncharacteristically, giggled.

Fiona looked askance at her husband. Ian, her Ian, Ian the minister, Ian the Rev, was talking about murdering someone. Not something she ever thought possible. She comforted herself by deciding he could not be serious; that they were just playing a game, albeit a drunken and rather distasteful one. Cool it, she told herself, don't be such an old prune, oops prude. Maybe I am a pruny prude or a prudish prune, she thought, as she also started to giggle. Ian thought she was amused by him.

Malcolm, who had been feeling a bit sidelined, offered to have Nigel come and stay with him so he could take care of the dreaded Samantha before she ran over any more innocent pedestrians.

"How old would Samantha be now, Simon? Do you think she might have smartened up?" Malcolm asked.

"I doubt it. She'd be in her late thirties or early forties, I think, but from what we've heard over the years she remains an egomaniacal, self-centred, daddy's darling, bitch."

"But other than that, she's okay," laughed Alison.

Nigel, loving the idea of staying with Malcolm, became starry-eyed. He turned to face Malcolm.

"Can I really visit you? Could we go to the Met? Can we do this while there is a Puccini opera playing? I've been wanting to see an opera there for years. I want to go to MOMA, and the Guggenheim, and the Natural History Museum. Could we fit that in Malcolm? Oh wow, the trip of my dreams with...." He stopped for a moment and his face fell.

"Except that Harrison won't be with me," he continued, his voice dropping. "We had always talked about New York. Harrison was most interested in the zoos. He had done a school project on zoos, and although he was not keen on the thought of animals being in cages, he really wanted to go to the Bronx Zoo to see the birds, and to do the jungle walk. Mostly he wanted to go to the Central Park Zoo because of all the conservation work they do there. And I also...." Nigel's wish list came to an abrupt end. "What am I thinking. I would murder this woman between visits to museums and the opera. Have I lost my mind?"

"Hey buddy, relax." Simon grinned at him. "This discussion is in the realm of the hypothetical. We're just blowing off steam here."

"Oh yes," I forgot. Well, pour me another glass of plonk and we can figure out how I can combine the opera where murders and death are common on stage with murdering the bitch off stage. Boy, am I ever soused."

"Okay, who's left?" Simon asked looking around the table. "Ah yes, you Justin. We don't have anyone yet to kill the vile pedophile."

"My husband the poet," giggled Alison, "the vile pedophile, the vile pedophile."

At this point, the host came to their table and politely asked them to tone it down since diners at neighbouring tables had complained about how rowdy they were getting.

"I think you all are way over your limits," said Justin looking both smug and disgusted. "How can you sit around joking and laughing about killing people? I don't know about the rest of you, but I came to Phuket to experience peace, not violence."

"You have a point Justin," Ian granted, somewhat chastened, "but we all seem to need some release, and other than maybe we have been a bit annoying to others eating here, we're just playing a game. We are joking, remember."

"Joking?" Simon asked. "Who's joking? Were you Ian, were you Nigel?"

"No!" they replied in unison. "Totally serious," agreed Ian.

"Can I bring you some dessert, or tea or coffee?" asked a very polite young server, clearly hoping they would either quieten down, or leave.

"Tea for all," Simon ordered, before the others had a chance to say anything. "I think we need to let the alcohol wear off a bit before we stagger back." The tea came with a plate of meringues which the server said were on the house.

They finished up, pooled their cash to pay the bill, and added a large tip to compensate for being such a nuisance. They walked back to the resort along the beach. There was no conversation. Each was wondering about the discussion. It was an incredibly warm and moonlit night, the white surf crashing in dramatic contrast to the ambient quiet of the beach. In the distance, the green lights on the overnight fishing boats started to appear. Were any of them serious? Were they just joking?

22

Saved by the Sting

Fiona woke up the next morning very confused. Her head felt like it was splitting in two, her mouth felt like it was full of the contents of her vacuum cleaner, and the room was spinning. Ian felt a bit nauseous but managed to get up and find coffee for them both.

"Is this what a hangover is?" asked Fiona. "Is this what the kids at uni found fun? I have never felt so awful in my life. Am I dying?"

"We finally did it," replied Ian. "I'm feeling rough too. I've never had that much alcohol, not even when I first moved to Halifax. It took a vacation for us to get drunk. How stupid is that. Just drink the coffee, and a few glasses of water, that, a shower and then a walk. We'll be okay."

Three hours later, after a long shower each, many cups of strong coffee, a couple of Aspirin pills, and some rolls, they were ready to go for a walk. Fiona was starting to feel more human and somewhat ashamed of herself. She replayed the evening's events to figure out how she got so out of control. She did not want that to happen again. Fiona suddenly stopped and turned to Ian.

"I just remembered the discussion last night. Did you actually agree to commit a murder, Ian?"

"I guess I did," Ian grinned, "but only in jest. No one was being serious Fiona, surely you realize that?" Fiona was not amused. On the contrary, she seemed quite agitated.

"You, a man of God, a church leader, would actually think it's okay to joke about killing someone? Are you crazy? I can't believe it. How would you talk to the kids if you heard them discussing how to kill someone that had upset them? Would you say ha ha ha, are you having fun kids?"

"Calm down, Fiona. Let's face it, each of the gang has suffered terribly, and unnecessarily, because of what those people did. They've all lost someone they loved very much just like we lost Heather. It's hard to understand and it hurts, you know that as well as anyone. Can you imagine how Nigel must have felt? His wife left him, he dedicated his life to his little boy who he adored, and then some irresponsible and probably sociopathic teenager kills him—on purpose or through unforgiveable carelessness. Think about what Justin went through. I wondered why he was so quiet. Poor guy. Can you imagine finding someone you love, someone you had planned to share your life with, dead from suicide? And that letter he told us about, I could cry. It makes me feel ill to think about what both she and he had gone through. And what about Alison and Simon? They seem to have raised a lovely, successful, and talented young woman only to have her mowed down by some spoiled drunken debutante. Her life just snuffed out as though it was meaningless. It just makes my blood boil. I don't understand God's plan in this, and I have trouble not feeling angry at God for allowing such suffering. But as Tennyson wrote, ours is not to reason why. Why these things happen is beyond our mortal comprehension."

He paused and took her hand.

"But Fiona, if it helps them to joke about committing murder; if its therapeutic, if it gives them even a moment of peace, I'm with them. And I am sure God would understand. Come on Fiona, you should be less judgmental, and more Christian." Ian sounded angry.

Holding hands, they walked along the beach in silence for a few moments.

"Ian," Fiona said sounding both sad and exasperated, "I have no memory of you like this. Why are you mad at me but okay with a group of people joking about killing? I get that you are angry and upset about all the losses, but not even after we lost Heather were you this weird about things. And I can sort of understand how you are feeling, but no way can I tolerate you agreeing to murder. In fact, if you take this any further...."

The threat was never finished. Someone was screaming. They stopped and looked around. Behind them, a woman was battling the surf trying to get out of the water. Twice she almost made it out, but the surf roared in and knocked her over. Ian dashed into the water to help her out, but on the third try she escaped the waves. As she emerged, Ian noticed that she had large red welts across her midriff and on one arm. She fell onto the sand crying and then vomited. Ian held her head while Fiona rushed to her side. They tried to calm her.

"It looks like a jellyfish got you. Let's get you up the beach.

There's a café just across the street and I'll get you some vinegar. That'll help until you get back to your hotel. You are staying nearby, are you?" The woman nodded. "You may need them to give you some antihistamine like Benadryl, especially if you are allergic. Fiona, you stay here with her and I'll get the vinegar as fast as I can."

Ian took off running as best he could across the soft sand. Fiona did her best to comfort the woman, who was suffering intense pain. "It burns so bad," she kept repeating. The welts grew brighter and more pronounced. Both women were pleased to see Ian coming back across the sand clutching numerous individual packages of vinegar.

Although the vinegar did little to ease the pain, it was enough that she was able, with the help of Ian and Fiona, to walk down the beach to the resort where she was staying. There, they took her straight to the first aid room. They stayed with her until they knew she was being taken care of and would be okay.

"That was more like the Ian I fell in love with," Fiona said, as they walked back. "You were so good with her. How did you know about using vinegar?"

"Before we came, I checked a few things about the area online and I noticed that there were often jellyfish, and that occasionally a swimmer was stung. Vinegar was a recommended emergency treatment for the sting. I also noticed it on a warning poster at the end of the beach to be careful since jellyfish were around. Thank God it wasn't a box jelly."

"A what?"

"Box jelly fish. They are huge translucent things that lurk

in shallow waters. They're sort of horror story creatures. They're incredibly toxic and there have been some deaths from them. I remember reading about a four-year-old who almost died after being stung in water only a foot deep. Interesting though, that was in Koh Mak and since then, the hotels have put up nets along the beaches to prevent the jellies from getting in. I don't think there have been any deaths on this beach. Here, tourists are more likely to get killed in vehicle accidents or by drowning. Or, of course, drinking too much." Ian grinned at Fiona. "Are you feeling better?"

"Yes, but I'm still mad at you," Fiona responded, "but I'll let it go for now cos I feel really proud of how you helped that poor lady,"

"Phew! Saved by the sting."

23

The Trolley Problem

"Hey guys," said Simon, the last to arrive at happy hour. He seemed agitated. "You'll never believe what I just found out."

It was almost a week since the drunken dinner when they had discussed murder. No one had broached the subject again, although Ian and Fiona were not alone in having had a heated discussion about the evening. Justin had expressed his disgust to Nigel, and Nigel had expressed his embarrassment at his enthusiasm for the murders to Malcolm. Simon had drawn comparisons to Hitler, but Alison stopped that quickly by reminding him of their no Hitler no Nazis agreement.

Simon stood by the table, too restless to sit down. "I just had an email from a friend at home and it seems that Samantha has done it again. This time, she drove her car into a parked car. They think she was chatting on her cell phone. I can't believe how many people are stupid enough to do that while driving. Anyway, it might have been okay if the car was empty. But there were two little kids in the back of the parked car. One of them is now in hospital with life-threatening injuries."

"And is rich and powerful daddy going to get her off again?" asked Nigel.

"Yup. Seems like he already did. That old geezer has always had more money than sense. My friend found out that it had been hushed up and settled with Samantha agreeing to pay the hospital bills for the family. He found out because another friend knew the family involved."

"I hope daddy didn't also get her another car," Ian said. "She's obviously a very dangerous driver."

"How does this keep happening? I don't get it." Fiona was visibly distraught.

"And will she also pay for the funeral if the child dies?" Nigel growled.

They sat in shocked silence. Simon went to the bar and got himself a glass of wine. He sat down on his return and took a large swallow.

* * *

"You know how we joked about criss-cross last week," he said, "well, I'm beginning to think there may be merit in killing someone like Samantha. She has no conscience, no morals and clearly doesn't give a damn about others. If her father wasn't so rich and powerful, she'd be locked up, but nope, she continues to endanger others' lives. What do you guys think? Is it moral to let people randomly kill through their stupidity, negligence, sexual perversions or whatever? If the law won't do anything, maybe people should." Simon was exasperated. "I've never really believed in vigilante justice before, but really." Alison put her hand on Simon's arm to calm him.

"Why don't we talk this through," suggested Alison, trying to distract him. I have an idea. "Have any of you heard of the trolley problem? We went over it in my ethics class, and I always remembered it. It was introduced by a female philosopher whose name I think was Fleet or Foot or something like that. I forget her first name, but I remember her thought experiment. Let's do it. Okay?"

"What do we have to do?" Malcolm asked.

"I'll present a moral dilemma story to you and we can discuss it. That's all. It'll be interesting if nothing else."

They nodded their consent. Justin looked particularly wary, but he agreed also. Ian and Fiona seemed the most interested.

"Right. Well here goes. To the best of my memory, here's the moral dilemma. There's this runaway trolley that is heading down tracks toward five guys who are working on the rails. If the trolley keeps going, it's probable that all of these guys will be killed. Now there's also another guy, let's call him Fred, who has control over a switch that can divert the trolley onto a different track. If he does that, it'll save the lives of the five workers, but the problem is there is one worker on the other track. If Fred does divert the trolley, the one worker will die for sure, but the five will be saved. The question is what should Fred do?"

"Glad I'm not Fred!" Justin said.

"Me too," Nigel agreed. "How long does he have to decide? This is pretty tough."

"I agree with you Nigel," Justin replied. "Can you guide us a bit, Alison?"

"Why is it so hard for you?" asked Ian. "Just think about what Jesus would say."

"What Rev?" asked Simon, sounding exasperated. There was a moment of silence.

"Okay," Alison said, ignoring Ian's comment and Simon's retort. "First, you need to realize that your decision would have to be almost instantaneous. The trolley is hurtling along, the guys are on the track. You can't rub your chin and philosophize for a few hours. Anyway, the key is not so much the decision itself, but how Fred makes the decision—what could he, or you, take into account to make the decision."

"But isn't it a simple binary choice?" Nigel asked. "He can either pull the switch or do nothing. Right?" The others nodded.

Malcolm, seeing the agreement, added in his most dramatic voice, "To pull or not to pull, that is the question; whether tis nobler in the mind to suffer the slings and arrows—." Multiple loud groans stopped him. They laughed.

"Okay, let's get back to it," said Alison. "Think about it this way. Choice number one: Fred could pull the switch and steer the trolley away from the five so that only one is killed. Now, he could do this either because he thinks that doing so would make five people happy, they survived rather than just one, or he could do so simply because he believes it's the kind of thing a good person would do. He wants to believe he is a good person. Got it?" They nodded.

"Okay, choice number two: Fred could let the trolley carry

on its path. He could do nothing. Maybe he would let the trolley carry on because he was thinking that something else could happen and the trolley would not end up killing the five people anyway. Or he could do nothing simply because it is always wrong to take an action that would kill another person. Every religion says killing is wrong, so he will not kill the one person even if it means that five others will die."

"That's what I was getting at," Ian interjected. "God makes these decisions, not us."

Seeing their faces, Alison continued, "Basically, you have to decide what you believe is the right thing to do, not just in terms of the action, but also in terms of the consequences. Are you more comfortable with the idea of doing what might be thought of as the right thing even if the outcome is awful, or of doing what you might think of as the wrong thing but with good, or at least less dire, consequences?"

"I don't know about the rest of you," said Nigel, "but I think I'd like some time to figure that out. Or at least to ask Google. It's an interesting dilemma alright, Alison, and not something I have ever thought about before. And I actually think it's worthy of serious reflection. What do the rest of you think?" The nods and thoughtful looks around the table gave Nigel his answer. "Can we give you our answer tomorrow night?"

"Of course, let's leave it for now. Why don't we take our drinks onto the balcony and admire the sunset? That's always easy. We'll talk some more tomorrow."

24

Thou Shalt Not Kill

Nigel got very little sleep that night. His first thought was that the question Alison asked was a no-brainer. Of course he would pull the switch. Why let five people die rather than one? But then he thought about what Simon had said about Samantha. Should she be killed to save others? How many deaths would she be responsible for if she continued to live freely in New York? From what Simon had told them, it seemed like she would never be held accountable, nor learn, nor feel remorse. What sort of an apology of a human being was she anyway? Did she deserve to live? Should she be the one to be killed to save others? Was the answer as easy as the moral dilemma story? It was much easier, he thought, to decide about a hypothetical situation that you knew you would never encounter, than one where it was possible for you to do the killing. Could he? Would he? Would he kill Miranda if he knew he could get away with it? He tossed and turned much of the night.

After a breakfast that was mostly coffee, Nigel walked around the resort until he found Malcolm. Although they had still not spent the night together, Nigel felt completely comfortable with Malcolm and was now sure that they would become life-long partners. He needed to discuss the killing issue with him. He wasn't surprised to find Malcolm beside one of the pools, still reading about the Met.

"Malcolm, are you interruptible? I really need to talk about what happened last night."

"Sure Nigel," Malcolm replied, putting his book down. "That was quite the discussion. I must say though, I love the thought of you coming to New York and the two of us going to the Met and the museums. That would be so great. I'm not so sure that I'm comfortable with the killing Samantha bit, though. At first, I thought everyone was joking, but it seems to be moving beyond that."

"Same, the killing bit is really getting to me." Nigel remained standing as he spoke. "You know, I thought it was all a joke too, and as a thought exercise it was rather interesting, but once I put it in the context of a real person, I took it seriously. Could I kill someone to save others? And if I could do that, could I kill for revenge? Would I kill Miranda? I do blame her for Harrison's death. I don't honestly know what I'd do given a chance. It's kind of scary. I'd love to get your thoughts."

"I thought about it too, it does get rather disturbing," said Malcolm. "I checked a few things online this morning to see if that would help. Why don't you tell me what are you thinking, and we'll go from there? But sit and relax a bit first."

Nigel told Malcolm that he had spent much of the night wondering if he could kill someone, and then thinking specifically about killing Samantha. Could he actually go to New York not just to be with Malcolm, but to kill a woman? On the one hand it felt like he could because he realized how dangerous she clearly was to the lives of others. But on the other hand, it was not an action that seemed possible for who he had always thought he was. It didn't fit with his sense of self, or his essential beliefs. He had been raised in the Anglican Church and had always believed "thou shalt not kill." And he had always taught Harrison how important it was to be kind to others.

He remembered, he told Malcolm, when Harrison had done a project for school about animals who kill. He smiled as he recounted how Harrison had asked him if animals were murderers. They had gone to the local library and found some books about which animals were most likely to kill and why, and of course, Harrison had done research online. He smiled as he remembered his discomfort when Harrison found information about black widow spiders killing their mates. He had not enjoyed explaining to Harrison what during or after sex meant. Malcolm chuckled. "And," he continued, "I so clearly remember when Harrison found out that the most murderous mammals were meerkats. It was not too long after we had watched the movie *Life of Pi*, and he had enjoyed the scene on the island when all the meerkats were what Harrison had described as "'popcorning'" up and down."

"I remember that scene too," Malcolm said. "It was amazing, they looked so incredibly cute."

"Yes, they sure did. Both Harrison and I fell in love with them. But in his research, Harrison found out that the dominant females routinely kill the offspring of the subordinate females in their group. Isn't that incredible! We had a lot of difficulty with that one. I remember Harrison asking if there were humans that did that." Nigel sighed heavily.

"You must miss him so much." Malcolm rested his hand on Nigel's arm.

"Every second of every minute of every day."

"I understand," Malcolm sympathized.

"I was also reminded of a movie I saw a couple of years ago. It was a thriller, which I don't usually like, but I went because Helen Mirren was in it and I think she's terrific." Nigel didn't want to focus on Harrison.

"Me too. Didn't you love her in *The Queen*?"

"She was fabulous. Didn't know you Yanks would watch that one."

The thriller, Nigel told Malcolm, was called *Eye in the Sky*. Malcom had neither seen it nor heard of it. It wasn't just a thriller, Nigel explained. It was also an exploration of the ethical challenges of drone warfare.

"Helen Mirren played a colonel who led a drone operation to capture terrorists. But she found out that they were planning a suicide bombing and so her mission changed from a capture to a kill. Everything was going okay until at the last minute a little girl entered the area. Here came the challenge. If they continued, they were sure that they'd kill the terrorists and stop the suicide attack. But they'd also kill the child, the little girl. But if they called off the attack, the terrorists would be able to carry out the bombing."

"So, what would you have done Malcolm? I spent a lot of last night wondering about the trolley question, and then the issue in the movie. I have no idea. I just kept going back and forth. Could I ever really kill someone? It's just not who I am. But what if it meant saving someone? Why would I refuse to save people—especially children? What would you do Malcolm?" he asked again. "What do you think most people do?"

"It is interesting, isn't it, Nigel. I've been wrestling with it as well. I had trouble sleeping last night too, so I got up and looked online to see if there was any info of relevance. I found some research done at Michigan State on the trolley dilemma but in an updated version. I read about it in a 2012 journal called *Emotion*. It was rather clever because they didn't just ask the question like Alison put it to us yesterday, they actually rigged up some kind of 3D simulation so the people doing it had to kinda live it."

"What do you mean? I don't get it."

"They had visuals and they had to act. They could see the trolley, no it was a train rather than a trolley, so they can see the train coming down the track toward the five people, and they can see there is only one person on the other track. They had a joystick. If they pulled it, they would re-route the train to save the five and kill the one on the other track. Or they could leave it alone and it would barrel down and kill the five."

"Wow! That's brilliant. So, what did most of them do?" Nigel interrupted Malcolm.

"More than ninety percent pulled the joystick."

Nigel was silent for a moment. "So much for thou shalt not kill."

25

Malevolent or Benevolent?

"Do you really believe it is possible to act in a way that is at once malevolent and benevolent?" Justin asked the group the next evening. "I have been thinking about the trolley dilemma you asked us about, Alison. It seems to be that pulling the switch could be seen to be benevolent in that you are saving five lives, but couldn't it also be seen as malevolent because you are causing the death of another person. This is really eating away at me; I just don't see how it's possible to make that kind of choice."

"I rather agree with you Justin," Nigel said, before Alison had a chance to respond. "Like I was telling Malcolm earlier, I was up most the night thinking about it, and I wondered how anyone could ever decide to kill when we all know at heart that killing is wrong. But the more I thought about it, the more I felt that there probably are circumstances in which I might well kill someone else."

"Like what?" asked Alison and Simon simultaneously.

"Well, suppose I had seen someone attacking Harrison. I think I would have killed to save Harrison. What I wondered about was whether I would feel the same if I saw someone attacking a child I didn't know."

Alison nodded. "Yes, you raise a good point, Nigel. I think most people would agree that a so-called crime of passion is one they are more comfortable with than one that is premeditated."

Fiona agreed. "You know even with the trolley question, there'd be emotion if not passion. But it wouldn't be premeditated. You wouldn't go out for a walk thinking that if you had a chance, you would kill one person to save five. Most people never think about stuff like that. I know I never have until you brought it up, Alison. It's the last thing I thought we'd be wondering about on a vacation!"

"So," asked Ian, looking rather agitated. "What if you recognized the one person on the track to be one of your friends or relatives? Would that really change how you would feel about pulling the switch? Actively doing something that you know will cause a death? Five strangers against one person you love. Why should one person you love," he said, stressing the you, "be more important than the others? Wouldn't the five also be loved, maybe not by you, but by their families, and after all, God loves everyone the same? I just don't agree with killing, and I don't think I could kill anyone under any circumstances. God taught us that murder is wrong, period."

"Nigel, let me ask you a follow-up question. How would you feel after you killed someone who was attacking Harrison? Would you simply be happy because Harrison was okay, or would you feel agitated because you had caused someone's death? The true source of happiness according to the Buddha is inner peace," Justin added. "How could you ever achieve inner peace if you know you have caused someone's death?"

"I think I need another drink," Nigel replied.

"I sort of agree with Justin," Simon said, "but I do think you need to take into account not just whether to murder or not, but what the consequences are. I have no doubt that I could kill a person if I knew that by doing so I would be saving the lives of others. And don't forget Justin, that the Dalai Lama endorsed the killing of Osama Bin Laden. I'm not so sure that Buddhism is that pacifistic."

Nigel returned with a full glass of red wine. "Anyone else need a top up?" he asked. Ian and Fiona were the only ones not to move. They sat in silence, each absorbed in thought, until the others returned to the table.

"Okay," Alison said, "it's time to take a vote. Remember last night I gave you options. Are you going to make your decision just on what's the right thing to do, or on the likely outcome? Ready? Let's start with Justin. How do you vote for the action, or for the consequence?"

"I say the most important consideration is the action and killing is always wrong. It's just not what a good person does."

"Nigel?"

"I keep going back and forth but I think ultimately I would have to agree that you do need to look at the consequences, and that sometimes killing just might be justified. But I reserve the right to change my mind."

"Rev?"

"I said it before, and I'll say it again. God teaches us that murder is wrong; the fate of others is in God's hands, not our own."

"Simon?"

"With all due respect to the Rev, I am not a believer, and I disagree. Sometimes you have to do things you might normally consider wrong, because the cost of not doing so is too great. As I said before, I cannot imagine letting five people die to save one even if it meant I had to kill the one. And to get back to the Buddha, I believe he said that if something is serious you have to take counter-measures. I believe that would be relevant here."

"And I agree totally with Simon," said Alison. "That leaves Fiona."

"And I agree strongly with Ian. It's up to God."

"Stalemate," Alison declared. "We have three for the action, and three for the outcome."

"Interesting. Now let's talk about something else. Anyone see the peacocks today? The one was displaying his magnificent tail feathers like I've never seen before. I felt kind of sorry for him, the peahen just gave him a sideways look and walked away."

"I saw and heard them," Justin replied.

"I did too," added Nigel. "Yes, the poor guys were in full mating mode, but the ladies were having none of it. Did you know that the males have harems of several females, and that they tend to gather in groups that are called parties?"

"Are you serious?" asked Justin. "Sounds like teenagers. By the way, I should tell you guys that I have decided to leave for Bangkok tomorrow. I'm not sure for how long. I'll be gone at least a couple of days, or maybe as much as a week. Anyway, I'm going to keep my room here while I'm away."

"Well, that's a surprise. What made you decide that?" asked Fiona.

"I have an aunt there who I've never met, and I need a break from you lot, and all this talk of sex and murder." Justin said grinning at them. "I'm off now to get ready, my flight is early. Bye all."

"Have a great time, Justin. Don't forget to go and see the emerald Buddha while you are there," said Malcolm.

"Have fun."

"Safe travels."

"See you soon."

"Bye."

They each wished Justin well.

"Oops, did I upset him? Was he being serious?" Alison wondered aloud. No one answered.

26

Justin's Break

Justin needed some time away from the gang. As much as he enjoyed the camaraderie, he found the discussion on murder disturbing, and he wanted a break from the nightly socializing. It seemed like the right time to have some time alone and to visit his aunt.

The flight left Phuket airport at eight-thirty. The drive to the airport took about ninety minutes, so Justin needed to be up extremely early and on the road by six at the latest. He relaxed on the drive in and enjoyed the scenery. The airport was not busy, especially in the area for domestic flights, and boarding was smooth and efficient. Unlike his trip from Vancouver to Phuket, this one turned out to be pleasant. The flight left on time, only took an hour and a half, and he was served a drink and a snack even though he was travelling economy. He was impressed.

When he arrived in Bangkok, Justin was not so sure that he had made the right decision. No longer were there the clear blue skies and sunshine of Phuket. In sharp contrast, everywhere was cloaked in a toxic smog. He wondered how anyone survived with such poor air quality.

Justin found a cab and set off to the Millennium Hilton.

He had booked a room there because the hotel was on the banks of the Chao Phraya River, and because it boasted breathtaking views over the city and the river, especially from the rooftop bar. Well, he thought to himself, Bangkok was breathtaking, but so far not because of any views.

Once in his room, he felt more relaxed. The air-conditioning was perfect. Given his early start and the pea-soup atmosphere, he stayed inside the hotel for the day. He had a swim in the pool, some lunch, and then read tourist brochures. The solitude was refreshing. He planned to take another day to himself before contacting his aunt. The next morning, he got up early and was delighted to see that the pollution levels were not as severe. He decided to dedicate the day to something he had only dreamed of before. After a light breakfast, he took a ferry to the Temple of the Dawn.

The river traffic was fascinating, and the view of the temple from the river was extraordinary. He felt his spirits soar. It was still early, so there was no long line-up of tourists at the entrance. He paid the small entrance fee, and, feeling like a little boy about to see Santa Claus, he entered what he thought must be the most mesmerizingly beautiful and architecturally stunning temple ever built. Ten hours and over a hundred photos later, Justin was on his way back to the hotel. He was utterly content. Sitting on the boat, he scrolled through the photos on his phone. He was especially pleased to see that he had captured the beauty of the pagodas, the gallery with the Buddha sculptures, and the three-headed elephant upon which was the God Indra. He found that fascinating and resolved to learn more about Indra. All he knew was that Indra was one of the more important figures in Buddhism.

That evening, Justin treated himself to a wonderful steak and lobster dinner in the hotel's fine dining restaurant. He decided that the day had been a turning point. It was not that he had stopped mourning Jennifer, but that he had now accepted the loss and was ready to move on. He felt like the peace of the temple had entered his soul. He would be okay. It was time to meet a relative. After dinner, he reached his aunt Samorn on the phone. She was stunned and delighted to hear from him and invited him to her home for dinner the next evening.

Justin spent the next morning exploring the area of Bangkok around the hotel, and the early afternoon enjoying the art displays at the nearby RCB Galleria. Unused to the degree of business, traffic noise, and visual stimulation, he was exhausted by mid-afternoon. He returned to his room for a rest before his visit.

Samorn lived alone in an apartment near the Chatuchak market. Justin asked the hotel concierge for directions and was pleased to learn he could easily get there by train. It was a pleasant journey. In response to his knock, the door was opened by a petite and exceptionally beautiful woman who looked years younger than the fifty-something he knew she was. She threw her arms around Justin and held him in a tight hug.

"Aunt Samorn, it's so lovely to be able to meet you."

"Call me Sam," she replied. "Come in and tell me all about you, and the family, and how you ended up on my doorstep."

"Would you like some tea?" she asked after they sat. "I don't have any beer or wine because I'm Buddhist, but I have some nice herbal tea, and dinner will be ready soon."

"Just water, thanks." Justin hoped dinner would be ready soon. The aroma that filled the room was very enticing, he was hungry, and he had discovered since being in Phuket that he adored Thai food.

In between mouthfuls of a delicious seafood curry with jasmine rice, Justin talked about the family, and life in Canada. Sam had stayed in touch with Justin's parents so had some knowledge of their lives, but she was full of questions about life in Toronto. She also expressed a strong interest in Justin's job and life in Vancouver. Not wanting to inject sadness into the evening, Justin omitted telling her about Jennifer, but he regaled her with stories of his students, and pulling his phone out of his pocket, showed her photos of the Vancouver beaches, Stanley Park, Granville Island, and the Whistler ski resort. Seeing the beauty of where he lived, she wondered why he was visiting in Thailand. He explained that he was on a break and wanted to go somewhere different. And of course, he wanted to meet his Thai family. He also delighted her by expressing his interest in Buddhism and raving about the wonderful day he had at the temple.

The evening passed quickly and, before it ended, they had made firm promises to keep in touch. Justin assured Sam that she would always be welcome in Canada, and that his parents would be thrilled if she could stay with them. Sam appreciated the invitation but explained that even though she worked forty-five hours a week as an assistant office manager of a hotel, her salary would never cover such a long trip. But they would see each other again, they felt sure. Many hugs and promises later, Justin was on the train going back to the hotel.

When he woke up the next morning, Justin felt even more at peace, but when he looked outside, the smog had returned. He decided he needed the fresh air of the coast and felt ready to return to the crazy gang of friends he had made. But he would come back to Bangkok. He didn't know when, but he had a powerful feeling that this trip was just an introduction to the city and the Thai members of his family. He booked a flight for the following day and spent his last day in Bangkok in his hotel room reading about Indra, and the history of Wat Arun.

27

Death and Persuasion

Landing at Phuket, it seemed to Justin that he had been gone for more than a few days. The experiences he had in Bangkok made it feel that way, he thought. He was pleasantly surprised at how delighted he was to be back. He hoped the rest of his trip would be relaxed with a more Zen-like mood than the dark feelings evoked by the discussions of murdering people. What a crazy group, he thought. He arrived back at the resort in time to freshen up and go to happy hour. He couldn't wait to talk about all he had seen and show them at least some of his photos. When he went in, Justin was surprised to see that Simon and Alison were not at the usual table. The rest of the gang greeted him warmly and asked about his trip. Justin had just started to tell them about Bangkok when Simon and Alison came in. They looked distraught.

"You're not going to believe this," Simon said, before he sat down. "Remember I told you about Samantha driving into a car that had kids in the back? Well, I just found out that the little girl that was in hospital died from her injuries yesterday. A beautiful little three-year-old girl. There was a photo of her on the net. It's just unbearable."

"Oh no," said Fiona. "That's so awful."

"God be with the family," added Ian.

"I can't believe this. First, our lovely Melody, and now this child whose life was barely begun. Who knows if there have been others in between? She has to be stopped," said Alison, wiping the tears that were running down her cheeks. "Someone, somehow, has to stop her before she kills more kids. Her damn father just bails her out each time and buys her another car. You'd think he'd stop by now; he must be at least seventy and she's not a kid anymore. That family is malignant."

"I think you are right." Nigel looked thoughtful. "This is too much to bear. That woman contributes nothing to society but pain and suffering. It's one thing to make a mistake as a teenager but as a middle-aged woman? But she gets away with it because of the family's money. They have no decency, no conscience. How many more families will lose a child or a spouse? How many more dads will have to go through what I have, and still am going through? You never get over the death of a child, especially a death caused by someone's carelessness." He sighed and wiped his eyes before continuing.

"You know, I have been thinking a lot about our criss-cross discussion. At first, I found the idea of killing anyone simply unthinkable, then as I thought about it and Harrison's death, it seemed possible. Now I am one step further. Hearing about this little girl just now, I have had enough. I think that I for one am ready for action. I actually do think it's time to kill the one to save the five, or however many more she is going to kill. I'm ready to pull the switch, Alison."

"Are you serious," Alison asked. "Are you actually saying

what it sounds like? You are really ready to go to New York and...."

"I can't believe I am saying this, but yes, at this precise moment I am."

There was a shocked silence.

"So," Alison said, "the unthinkable went to the possible, and now it's on its way to action. Wow. I'm stunned, I really only meant it all to be hypothetical."

"Does this mean we have to do something about, or should I say to, Miranda?"

"No," replied Nigel. "I am not making my action contingent on that, it's up to you and your conscience."

"Well, let us think about it; it does seem only fair. Crisscross, right?"

"Count me out," Justin quickly added.

"And us," Fiona said. "No way are Ian and I going to be part of this. I can't believe we are sitting here, among the privileged, enjoying drinks in the beautiful place, and plotting to do the worst thing a person can do to another. A heinous sin."

"In fact," Ian added, "let's go Fiona. I can't be part of this, I think I need some space." He stood up. Fiona followed.

"No, don't rush off like this, Rev," Alison replied. "I totally understand how you feel and where you are coming from. You are a good man. And you, Fiona, are a good woman. I know that both of you would do whatever you could to help anyone, and certainly to protect someone who was in danger of being killed."

"Yes, of course we would," Fiona replied as she and Ian sat back down hesitantly.

"Then we are not really in disagreement, are we?" Alison questioned them.

"Well, no, not when you put it that way. But no way will Ian or I ever agree to kill anyone."

"Of course not, but you would protect someone in danger, wouldn't you? All we are really talking about is a way to protect innocent people—especially children—from being hurt. I can't imagine people as kind as you two, or as gentle as Justin, refusing to help protect people who are in danger of being killed."

Justin looked a bit confused. Ian and Fiona looked uncomfortable.

"I would never refuse to help a child. I am a strong proponent of children's rights, and that includes their right to be protected from all forms of violence. I have worked with children and youth for years, and after what happened to Jennifer, I am acutely aware of how easily and profoundly they can be hurt." Justin said, with as much indignation as he could muster.

"Well, I guess that's how we feel too isn't it, Ian? We feel the same as Justin." Fiona was impressed with Justin's statement and vehemence.

"Okay, I have an idea," said Alison, after a few moments of silence. "Since we all agree on the importance of protecting children, let's exchange information about Miranda, Samantha, Alexander, and Jennifer's uncle, sorry I forgot his name, and then see what happens after we each go home."

"It's Blake." Justin sounded much calmer.

"I think you two go home in a couple of days, right Rev?

So how about tomorrow night we'll exchange written information about these people, and if we continue to agree on the importance of protecting children, we can sort out more details on an as-needs basis later. The time may come when we have to decide whether to do something to make sure children are protected from these folks."

Justin, Ian, and Fiona, relieved to have ended the conflict amicably, agreed. Ian wished to ensure the tension was dissipated.

"Let's go out on the balcony and admire God's nightly handiwork. Look at that incredibly beautiful sky tonight." They each followed Ian outside.

That night, as they were preparing for bed, Simon asked Alison how she had diffused the situation so easily and got the three holdouts to change their minds. "I'm not even sure that they realized what they agreed to," he said.

She grinned at him. She explained that she had recalled from one of her psychology classes that there are three key actions you need to take to change someone's mind.

"First, instead of telling them they are wrong, you tell them you understand their perspective. Second, you suggest a solution by reframing the issue. What I tried to do tonight was to get them to think about protecting children rather than killing someone. They sort of have to agree, don't they? And third, and just as important, is that you must allow them to keep their dignity, to save face, while changing their opinion."

"Geez Alison. Is that how you have been manipulating me to agree to everything you wanted all the years?"

"Of course, my darling. Good night."

28

Nigel Returns Home

The last night of Nigel's stay he spent with Malcom. Being intimate with Malcolm left Nigel feeling overwhelmed with a degree of contentment and desire that he had never felt before. He felt more joy than he had since Harrison's birth. He felt more at peace than he had since Harrison's death. He lay in bed after they had made love for the second time that night and recalled something his introductory psychology professor had told the class about Freud. Freud had noted that sometimes men were quite impotent with their wives, but sexually unimpeded with their mistresses. It was, according to Freud, the prof had explained, due to Victorian women being fragile creatures who must be treated very carefully. What stuck in Nigel's mind was that Freud had explained that men could not lust where they loved, nor could they love where they lusted. Love and sex were separate. You loved your wife and lusted after your mistress.

Nigel reflected on how, until this night, he could not love where he lusted. He had loved his wife during her pregnancy and for a while after Harrison was born. He had only lusted after male strangers. What an incredible experience it was to be free to love and lust the same person. He turned to Malcolm, wondering if he was up for more sex. No pun intended, he chuckled to himself. But Malcolm was asleep with a smile on his face.

Malcolm's flight was leaving early, but Nigel accompanied him to the airport. They got up at four-thirty. The previous day they had ordered two to-go breakfast bags; they picked these up from the front desk on their way to the cab. On the hour and half drive they sat quietly, hand in hand. It would be difficult parting today. But they would see each other within a few months. They had planned that Nigel would stay with Malcolm in New York for a month, then Malcolm would fly to England to stay with Nigel. Then they would decide where to live, but they knew it would be together. Malcolm was confident it would be in England. He was ready for a complete change.

Nigel stood by while Malcolm checked in at the Bangkok Airways Desk. His flight was on time. In the time they had before Malcolm needed to go through passport control and final security, they sat together and ate the fruit and cereal bars and drank the juice from their breakfast bags.

"I feel like a little kid on a school picnic," Malcolm said, as he wiped the crumbs from his pants.

"Here," replied Nigel, "let me put all this stuff in the garbage pail and then I'll walk with you to security."

A final hug, a final kiss, and Malcolm disappeared among the many travellers heading into final screening before boarding their aircraft.

Nigel felt sad to see Malcolm go, but secure in their love for each other and the knowledge that he would see him again in a little over three months. Back outside the airport, he got a cab right away. He dozed all the way back to the resort. After a second breakfast with lots of coffee, he determined he would enjoy the last week of his time there. It would go fast enough, he believed, and he had a lot to do as soon as he got home. His priority would be finishing his manuscript. He wanted to finish it before he went to New York, by which time it was due at the publisher anyway.

* * *

As he expected, Nigel's last week did pass quickly. He spent a great deal of time walking the beach while thinking about his manuscript. One day, he took a longtail boat ride to Freedom beach, where he swam in the warm and deep blue water and enjoyed a lunch before returning. He went shopping to find some sort of souvenir for Quentin. Sooner than he would have thought possible, it was time to say goodbye to Ian and Fiona, Simon and Alison, Justin, and the staff in the lounge who had been so helpful and friendly throughout his stay. It had been a good month, he thought, as he packed, and it had promise of much good to come. He was thrilled he had come, and maybe he and Malcolm would come back together sometime. For now, he was looking forward to getting home, and starting the next stage of his life with his new partner.

Nigel's flight was uneventful and smooth other than the usual turbulence and circling before landing in London. His friend Quentin was waiting for him at the arrivals area at Heathrow Airport. As he drove Nigel home, Quentin shared good news about the hedgehog Nigel had rescued. Hazel, as the vets had named her, had recovered fully and had been released back into the wild. Quentin also shared that he was madly in love. Kate had come to work with him as an interning veterinary student. She had wanted to rehabilitate wildlife since she was a young child and was so moved by hand-rearing some of the orphans at the clinic that she cried, Quentin told Nigel.

"She sounds like your perfect soulmate, and guess what, I met mine, too. What were the chances, but there at the resort was my Malcolm. Quentin, I have never felt like this before. Isn't love just the most incredibly amazingly wonderful...."

As Nigel gushed on, Quentin listened with amusement and delight. By the time they reached Nigel's home, Quentin had heard all the details, including how fantastic Malcolm was in bed.

After a day of adapting and recovering from the flight, Nigel focused on his manuscript. He had a moment of panic when he first turned on his computer and couldn't see the file on the desktop where he thought he had saved it. It was there. Calm down, he told himself. He was eager to add a chapter on the phenomenon of the ladyboys in Phuket. It would replace the section on pederasty. He needed to go through the photos he had taken and select one or two to include. He also wanted to do some research to learn about the social history of the ladyboys, and whether there was anything comparable in other parts of Asia or elsewhere. Within two days, he had finished the book and sent it to the publisher.

With the book complete, he focused on home improvements. Everything had to be perfect for when Malcolm came.

Nigel hired a renovation company to update the kitchen, and an interior designer to re-furnish the bedroom. One thing that did look good, he decided, was the garden. He was pleased with the gardener's choice of shrubs and flower beds, and the upkeep of the lawns. Having reflected on all that needed to be done before he went to New York, he figured out the earliest date he could leave. After a Skype call with Malcolm, he had a confirmed date. He booked his flight. Almost everything was set. What they had not talked about was the killing of Samantha. Neither was sure about what to say. Were they serious? Was that really the reason for the trip? Would they actually go ahead?

29

Ian and Fiona Leave

A few days after Nigel flew back to London, it was time for Fiona and Ian to leave. Disturbed by the conversation with the gang, Ian and Fiona had a sleepless night before their flight. Fiona continually went over and over what had been said. She worried that Ian, and maybe even she, had agreed that there were times when killing was okay. Did she know who Ian was anymore? Was she over-reacting? Fiona was conflicted. Ian was feeling ashamed. He was a minister, a man of God. He was angry with himself at not being more forceful about how wrong murder was under any circumstances. Why were they spending time with people who seemed to enjoy talking about murder? That was not what they had gone away for. They both tossed and turned all night.

Getting back to Halifax was gruelling. They first had to fly to Bangkok, then to Doha where they had three-hour layover, then to Montreal where they had a five-hour layover before the final leg to Halifax. To add to their misery, the flight between Bangkok and Doha was very turbulent. Moderate turbulence, the pilot had called it. That's an understatement, thought Fiona. To make matters worse, the child sitting behind Ian was crying, and the woman sitting across the aisle was vomiting. It was definitely time to pray, Ian thought. Fiona checked her watch. Two more hours to Doha. She had never imagined being in Qatar, she thought. At least they had three hours between flights to find their departure terminal. She was nervous about all the transfers. She was so tired and had hardly any sleep the night before and...stop thinking this way, she told herself. How did their much-anticipated relaxing vacation turn into such a nightmare, she wondered.

* * *

As their fourth flight finally descended to Stanfield International Airport, Fiona felt her muscles begin to relax. She looked out at the fog and thought we made it; we're home. Beside her, Ian was sleeping. They had barely spoken throughout the flights. Fiona was unused to feeling such tension within her, or between them. Her unease added to the emotional and physical exhaustion that enveloped her. The descent was characteristically bumpy, and Ian awoke.

"Home?"

"It seems so." Fiona replied coldly, wondering why she felt such antipathy to the man she had loved so intensely before the trip. Maybe once she had some sleep, she'd feel better, she thought.

After a fourteen-hour sleep both were feeling better, and they were keen to get the children. The reunion was joyful. Lachlan, Caitlin, and Maggie regaled them with stories about things that had happened in their absence. There were lots of stories about Benji, Aunt Erin's rambunctious ever-affable golden retriever. Maggie had dressed Benji in one of her dresses, and Aunt Erin had taken pictures. Benji had run away. Benji had brought home one of the neighbour's chickens. Benji had eaten Aunt Erin's necklace, and then vomited it up. Benji had happily buried a chew bone thinking it was a real one. They begged for a dog of their own. Ian and Fiona distracted them, at least temporarily, with their souvenirs.

That evening, after lots of hugging and kissing and all three children were asleep, they sat together at the kitchen table with their coffee. Fiona said those four words many men hate to hear: "We need to talk." Ian agreed. They reviewed the reason for the trip; had it helped them heal from the tragic loss of Heather? In that it had provided a distraction and made them appreciate the intense joy of their family and daily life, it had. But in that they had ended up with the semi-philosophical focus on justifications for murder, and tension between them, it had not.

"But did we have a good time at all?" Fiona asked.

"We should not lose sight of all the good things. We enjoyed some gorgeous scenery and sunshine, and even though I was nervous about trying the food, I actually came to love it, spices and all."

"We also got into good shape," Fiona interrupted. "What with those long walks on the beach and swimming in the pools, I think I may have lost a couple of pounds despite all the rice and noodles."

"And we had some enriching side trips. And, of course, we did meet some remarkably interesting people," Ian added with a sly grin.

Ian reached across the table and took Fiona's hands. "Let's

not let what happened those last few nights spoil things. We were blessed to have this opportunity to experience a different part of God's world, and to come back safely to our wonderful life here. You don't need to worry about me murdering anyone Fiona. I would never do that no matter what. And," he added, "I love you. I would never do anything to disappoint you."

"I love you too Ian, and I am sorry if I distrusted or insulted you. You know, I think a lot of my angst has been from thinking that maybe I could kill someone if they were threatening Lachlan, Caitlin, or Maggie. But I will put my trust in God to guide me to always do the right thing."

Moving around the table, Fiona kissed Ian. He responded with more passion that she had anticipated.

"Hang-on," she said, "let's at least open the mail before we go to bed."

"If you insist." Ian smiled, gave her a perfunctory kiss, and got the pile of mail that had arrived during their absence.

They didn't open the bills until the next day. That reduced the pile by more than half. Most of their personal mail came by email, but occasionally there would be something in snail mail. Ian had a letter from an old friend from high school who he had not seen nor heard from for a long time.

"This is interesting." He told Fiona who the letter was from. "Remember Coran—you met him at our wedding—he has written to tell me that his niece has just been accepted into Dalhousie engineering, and that he is running for the NDP in Cape Breton. I wonder why he didn't email this."

Fiona had been opening a couple of pieces of mail addressed to her and only partly heard what Ian said.

"Oh my," she said, jumping up from the table waving a letter that had been forwarded from her office in Halifax. "I have been invited to give a keynote address at a social work conference in Vancouver. The theme is issues in child protection. They are offering to pay all my expenses Ian. Oh wow," she read on, "it's at the Westin Bayshore, and it says that it's right by the seawall near the downtown, and near Stanley Park. This is amazing!"

"When is it?'

"Let me see. It's in May. I have to let them know right away. How can I let this chance go Ian, but how can I, or we, leave the kids again so soon? We just got back! After never leaving Nova Scotia, are we really going to go away twice in one year?"

Ian thought for a few moments before he spoke.

"I have a solution. Let's all go. You, me, and the three kids. It won't hurt for Caitlin and Lachlan to miss some school. Let's blot out the bad feelings we came home with by having a real family holiday in Canada. The weather's great in Vancouver in May. Remember Justin talked about how beautiful it is there, and we have never stayed as a family in a hotel. The kids will be fascinated by how different that is from camping. Your way is paid. I can cash in some savings, and what the heck, we'll use the charge cards. It'll be perfect."

"But it is a safe place to take the children?" Fiona asked, "It's a big city. There's homeless folks, and drug addicts on the streets."

"They'll be fine, Fiona." Ian stopped her. "Sure, it has the usual challenges of a city but remember Justin saying it was a great place for kids. There's lots for them to see and do well away from the scarier parts of the downtown. And anyway, just think, it gives us a good reason to put off getting the kids that puppy they all begged for today."

"Okay, I'm sold. Let's do it."

"Yes ma'am," Ian grinned. "Let's do it now. Get out of those clothes and onto the bed before I take you in the kitchen in a very non-ministerial way. Love not murder, love not murder," he sang, to the tune of "Love and Marriage," as they headed upstairs.

30

Alison's Plans

If you must go home, this is the way to do it, Alison thought, as the plane levelled off after takeoff. Ah, the joys of travelling business class, she thought, stretching in the spacious pod, sipping her champagne, and scrolling through the movies. The first run ones she had either seen or was uninterested in, so she moved to the comedy section. Simon, who was sitting in the pod across the aisle from her, heard an amused shriek. He was about to read the memoir *Hitler's Stolen Children* which he hidden from Alison at the bottom of his suitcase and kept for the flight home. Distracted, he looked across at her.

"Simon," she said, sounding surprised, "look what movie is playing. Is this a sign? It's *Throw Momma From the Train*. Do you believe it?"

"Criss-cross," he replied wryly, and turned back to his book.

Once home, they checked dates with Michael and Amy, and bought tickets for their trip to London to see the grandchildren. Alison had wanted to fly business again, Simon thought economy would do. They compromised on premium economy. Alison then investigated means of homicide. Although not entirely sure they were being serious, she and Simon had agreed that given the circumstances, they would carry out their plan. Miranda and Samantha, they believed, were the most dangerous of all the criss-cross targets.

How to commit the murder was the issue. They realized the irony of them both having spent their careers studying murders while neither had a clue how to go about committing one. Alison usually asked Google search if she had a question. Google, she had found, was not only omnipotent, but had great answers to questions like what to cook for dinner, or where to go on vacation. She remembered reading some time ago that people also turned to Google to ask if they were fat, if they were pregnant, and even where they left their keys. She doubted even Google could answer that other than to suggest that the keys were likely where they had been put. But how to get away with murder was probably not a good question to search using Google. All she knew was that since the murder would take place in England, she couldn't use a gun. She wouldn't be allowed to have one in her luggage, and they were too difficult to access there. Poison was likely more practical, she thought.

Alison recalled hearing about a woman in France who had asked Google which was the best poison to use to kill someone and how to poison someone without getting caught. In all her searching she had apparently missed the advice, "If you kill someone, don't Google how to do it first." By the time she killed her husband, the search log was extensive, and it included the method she used. She had made it easy to be charged with first degree murder. Alison would not repeat that error.

The safest approach, Alison decided, was to use the computer lab in the science department of the university. She would look up toxins as though she were a student of biology or chemistry. After a few false starts, she found what she thought was her answer. Ethylene glycol, better known as antifreeze, she read, was not only used in suicides, but also was the number one homicidal poison in the US. People had used it to kill neighbours' pets, and neighbours. It was, she read, colourless and odourless, and had a slightly sweet taste. Better yet, it was available online from multiple retailers. Alison could feel her blood pressure and temperature rising with the excitement she was feeling. This was it, the answer. They would find out which pubs Miranda went to—didn't everyone in England go to pubs?—and then find a way of slipping antifreeze into Miranda's drink. Sitting still was now difficult, so Alison left the lab to go for a walk both to calm herself, and to think the option through further.

Walking across the lawn toward the faculty club, Alison wondered if they could take some antifreeze on the plane. She did not know if it was flammable, or if it might be a disallowed substance, even in checked luggage. But surely they would also sell it in England, she thought. She now felt an urgency to return to the computer and find out if she would be able to obtain antifreeze in England. Still wary of being discovered, she used the search term "ethylene glycol poisoning in Europe." There was nothing specific on England, but in reading the abstracts of a few articles that came up, it seemed clear that it was available there. She continued her search to confirm this. What came up next put an immediate and crashing end to her excitement. To avoid accidental poisonings and its easy use in homicides, she learned, antifreeze was sold with an additive that gave it a bitter taste. There goes that one, she muttered to herself, and decided to have a lunch break.

Given the disappointment of the morning, she treated herself to an upscale lunch at the faculty club. One prawn and avocado salad, and two glasses of Sauvignon Blanc later, Alison was ready to continue her search. Thinking about how Miranda had killed Harrison by feeding him something he was allergic to, she wondered if there could be a way she could get Miranda to ingest something toxic. She pictured Miranda being offered a foxglove flower by a stranger who said it was delicious. She chuckled at the absurdity of the thought but looked up toxic plants anyway. Perhaps something would be come up and perhaps she would be inspired. It did and she was.

The seeds of the castor bean plant, she discovered, contain ricin. And according to the Centers for Disease Control, ricin is one of the most toxic biological agents known. The flowering shrub, she learned, is grown throughout the US as an ornamental annual. The seeds, readily available at garden shops, are not toxic unless chewed, or used to create a fine powder. When Alison read that, it triggered a memory of Donald Trump receiving a letter that was thought to contain ricin. She'd ask Simon when she got home, since it was the sort of thing he would know. She read further. Eights seeds, if chewed, would be enough to kill an adult. If this was the answer, they would have to find a way to get Miranda to chew eight seeds, or they would have to make a powder from them and get her to ingest the powder.

"Simon," she called, when she got home. "I need to tell you about what I found out today. I may have the answer on how to carry out our criss-cross project." She filled Simon in on what she had learned. "Wasn't it ricin that was in the letter sent to Trump?" she asked him.

"They thought it was at the time," Simon replied, "but they found out later that the sender screwed up—well, depending on your perspective. Instead of sending the actual ricin, they had just put the seeds in the envelope. If you put ricin powder in an envelope, it becomes airborne when the envelope is opened, and the poor soul who opens it probably inhales the ricin. But the seeds would have to be eaten. Do you remember, Alison," he continued, "both George W. and Obama were sent envelopes with ricin in them. I think someone was charged in each case, but I can't remember the details."

"Mmmm," Alison mused, "if it's that popular a way of getting rid of presidents, then Miranda will be in good company if we use it."

31

Justin's Retreat

Peace at last, Justin thought to himself. He was the last of the gang still in Phuket. Since Simon and Alison had left two weeks ago, he had relished the time alone. He had looked into several yoga classes in the area and decided on one in Kata that offered sessions in Bikram yoga. He found the experience intense but therapeutic. He had also attended a free meditation class at the Dharana Meditation and Retreat Centre. He found it so helpful he spent four of his last ten days in Thailand at one of their retreats.

The retreat promised to release stress and cultivate a sense of wellbeing. He couldn't think of anything he wanted more. Each day began at six with some sort of excursion and individual training. It took some getting used to, having to be up and active for three and half hours before the breakfast. The morning was free between breakfast and lunch, and most days Justin used that time to read, go for walks, and think about what he wanted to do when he returned to Canada. The afternoons passed quickly with a variety of yoga and meditation practices. After dinner there was free time again, but Justin usually was too worn out to do anything but fall asleep early.

His favourite part of each day was the morning excursion.

The group would visit a different beach or forest area each morning where they would have some tea, teachings, and meditation sessions as the sun rose. As much as he hated having to get up at five-thirty in the morning, he found each morning's excursion filled him with a peacefulness and joy that had been absent in his life since losing Jennifer.

Justin returned to the resort feeling refreshed and rejuvenated. He was now ready to go home. But he could not bear the thought of returning to Vancouver, and despite having decided not to pursue any other family connections in Thailand, he found he really missed his parents. He realized, while at the retreat, that what he needed for the time being was to be with his family in Toronto. There he would think about where to apply for a new teaching job. He missed his time in the classroom, and his students. It had also become important to him to continue the Buddhist practices that had so helped him over the past weeks. Searching online, he found a Theravada Buddhist community in Toronto. Better yet, it was in the downtown area near the university, a location that was easily accessible by subway from his parents' home. He decided he would go there the first Sunday after his return. Maybe he would meet some like-minded people, he thought, and at the very least, it should facilitate his continued practices of mindfulness and meditation.

Landing in Toronto, Justin was reminded of how grey and flat the area was. It seemed especially so after the intense colour and lush vegetation of the Phuket area. But it was home. The flight had been smooth with all connections on time. It was a vastly different experience from the chaotic and long flight he had endured getting to Phuket. His luggage rolled down the chute among the first bags, and he did not need to line up or wait for a cab to his parents' house. Approaching the city on the characteristically busy Gardiner Expressway, he practised one of the mindfulness techniques he had learned. He first stroked each finger of his left hand with his right index finger and then his right hand with his left index finger. That helped him feel relaxed until he noticed the ever-increasing cost of the cab ride. He stroked each hand again.

His parents rushed out as soon as the cab pulled up at their house and enveloped him in hugs and kisses. They had a bottle of excellent red wine, a meal, and his childhood bedroom ready. Despite being exhausted, he was feeling too restless to sleep so took each offering in order. The wine was dry and smooth, and the jerk chicken, rice and peas were his favourite comfort food. Two hours passed as they ate, drank, and talked about his trip. No one mentioned Jennifer, but there were many questions about if he had eaten well, if he was sleeping okay, and whether he was feeling better. Justin summarized his trip. He left out the conversations about killing people, mentioning the gang very briefly. He focused on his visit to Aunt Samorn in Bangkok, and taking his phone from his pocket, he showed his parents photos of her. He promised to show them the rest of the photos the next day.

The combined effects of the long flight, the wine, and food, could no longer be ignored. Justin hugged his parents good night and went upstairs to his old room. On the dresser sat the ragged teddy bear he had owned since infancy. He could not resist putting Ted on the pillow. He reached into the back pocket of his jeans to remove his phone which he had put there after showing his parents the photos of Bangkok and Sam. A piece of paper fell out with the phone. Alison and Simon had given it to him on the last night the gang was all there. How could he have forgotten, he wondered.

Criss-Cross Targets was written at the top of the piece of paper. Under that was the name Alexander Santos, and an address in Wellington. Wellington was a small semi-rural area north of Halifax, Fiona had told Justin. Alexander was Justin's assigned target. An assignment he had adamantly refused to accept. Nonetheless, like Ian and Fiona, he had accepted the information to end the discussion. It had been the last night the gang met in the lounge. Overall, the atmosphere at their table in the lounge had been cordial. Most of the discussion had centred on the highlights of the trip for each of them. But then Simon had suggested that they meet up again in a year and see if their project, as he called his plans for four murders, had been successful. In the meantime, he said, they should not contact each other at all. They could further protect themselves by having nothing recorded digitally.

"And so," Simon said, "I have for each of you the information you need on paper."

Ian, Fiona, and Justin were shocked that Simon continued with this insane suggestion. It was one thing to have hypothetical discussions, but this was going too far. This is one game of Simon Says, Fiona had muttered, that I am not playing. But they each took their note to maintain the peace.

Justin threw the note down, finished undressing, and fell

into bed. He turned to Ted who was still on the pillow. You get it Ted, he thought. You could never hurt anyone, and neither could I. With that comforting thought, Justin fell into a peaceful sleep.

PART 3: AFTER
April-September 2018

32

Justin

During his first week home, Justin did little other than go for walks and reflect on the changes in his life over the past two years. He had settled into a new job in Vancouver, a job and a city he had loved. He had met and planned to spend his life with Jennifer, a woman he had loved deeply. All that was taken from him. He had gone to Thailand which, upon reflection, he decided had been wonderful and terrible, invigorating and tiring. Seeing the temples and learning more about Buddhism had been inspirational. Meeting his aunt had given him a sense of belonging and being cared for. The conversations about murder had been disconcerting. He wondered how people who were so well educated and socially pleasant, like the professors, could actually plan to commit murder. And even Nigel, who had initially seemed like a typical reserved and uptight English noble, had agreed that murder was sometimes okay. Thank goodness for the Rev and Fiona, he thought. Good to know I was not the only one who found the idea of any murder, even joking about it, abhorrent. What now, he wondered.

Walking down Yonge Street, Justin recalled how much he disliked Toronto. Much as he loved his family, he could not imagine spending his life among the street kids on Yonge, or the suits on Bay Street, or the greyness of the city, the density of the buildings, the lack of trees in the downtown, and a lake that could never appeal like the Pacific Ocean. The best part of Toronto, he decided, aside from its wonderfully multicultural make-up, was the airport. It provided easy access to much of the world. But where would he go and what would he do? He needed trees and grass to think, and so he walked down to Queens Quay, and caught the ferry to Centre Island.

Fifteen minutes after boarding the ferry, Justin was walking along past the fountains and amusement park toward the Gibraltar Lighthouse. He recalled the lighthouse from his childhood. There were many stories about it being haunted by the ghost of the first lighthouse keeper back in the early 1800s. He smiled to himself as he remembered one of his teachers telling the class about how the lighthouse keeper was murdered, and so returns each summer to haunt the lighthouse. As a young boy, Justin thought it would be cool to see or hear this. Now he just felt haunted. He assumed it was from the anxiety of not knowing what to do, or where he belonged. As he walked, he made a mental list of what he missed and tried to figure out what he wanted.

What he missed, he decided, was simply everything. He missed his apartment in Vancouver, he missed his job. He even missed the crazy kids who asked questions about genital waxing. He missed his fellow teachers. And more than anything he missed Jennifer and the glorious feeling of being in love and having that love reciprocated. Though he had accepted losing her, he still missed her. He realized he even missed

Phuket. There, he'd had new things to do and learn, and people to meet. He'd enjoyed the sunshine, the walks along the beach, the friendly staff, the fresh mangoes, and especially the few days he spent at the Buddhist retreat.

So, he asked himself, what can I learn from this list about a future direction? He realized he would first have to accept that he could not get back what he had lost when he lost Jennifer. Would he ever experience such love again, he wondered? He could not imagine doing so, but he told himself, anything is possible, and after all he did have an uncle who fell in love and married in his late sixties.

He noticed fewer families around and realized that he had walked well away from the amusement park on Centre Island to Ward's Island. Time for a break. He stopped at The Rectory because it had a pleasant outdoor patio with several trees around. He ordered a salad and a craft beer. While he ate, he thought further about what he missed this time adding the question of what he could do about it.

A job and an apartment seemed like the easiest things to get back, but where he had no idea. He did not speak French so did not want Montreal, did not like living in Toronto, and could not imagine living in Vancouver without Jennifer. He thought about Halifax, but although it was on the ocean and there were beaches, what he had heard about the climate and the lack of cultural activity from Ian and Fiona did not make it seem appealing. As much as he enjoyed nature, he needed to be in or close to a major city, and preferably by an ocean. He decided to look for teaching positions over the next couple of months and see if any appealed. Perhaps he would let job availability determine his city.

Unlike teaching, his missing of Buddhist practices could be dealt with now. Despite his interest in attending the downtown Toronto Buddhist Community, he had yet to go. He determined that he would attend next Sunday, five days away. That, he decided, would be step one on a path to real healing.

He noticed Elaine at his first meeting. She came in with her own meditation mat which she placed next to his. As he looked up, she smiled at him with her large hazel eyes reflecting inner contentment. His visceral reaction discomforted him. The last thing he had expected to feel when entering the meeting room was sexual desire. But he could not ignore the reality. He felt guilty and confused. What would Jennifer think? How could he feel this way for a woman he had not even met? What was happening to him? He tried his best to concentrate on the mediation he was supposed to be, and had intended to be, engaged in. It was much harder than he expected. He eventually managed to calm down and focus, and he participated in the mindfulness exercises without a problem.

At the end of the morning session, he joined the group for lunch. He noticed an empty chair next to Elaine and could not resist heading directly toward it.

"Er, mind if I sit here," he asked awkwardly.

"Please," she replied, with a warm smile. "Is this your first time here? I'm Elaine by the way."

"Justin, and yes."

"I've been coming here since I got back from Thailand, about a month ago."

"You were in Thailand?" Justin exclaimed, forgetting his nervousness.

"I spent two years there teaching English as a second language to eight- and nine-year-olds and I loved every minute of it. The kids were amazing. That's where I learned about Theravada Buddhism. I plan to go back there next year as long if I can get another position. I needed to be home for a while to see my parents. My dad's been sick."

For a moment, Justin was speechless. Was this really happening or was he having an amazing dream from which he would awaken depressed. He was tempted to pinch himself. Instead, he told Elaine about his recent trip. He left out the upsetting incidents.

"But don't you want to go back?" Elaine asked.

"You're not going to believe this Elaine. But I am a teacher too. I quit my job in Vancouver for reasons I don't want to go into right now, and I have been wrestling with where to apply for a new job. Is Thailand a real possibility? I would love to go back. I loved it, the people, the lushness, the flowers, the climate, and I have family there that I still haven't met. How do you go about getting a job there? That just might be what I am looking for."

"Would you like to go for a walk now that lunch is finished? I'll fill you in on the details."

Justin readily agreed and as they left together, the last line spoken in *Casablanca* came into his mind: I think this is the beginning of a beautiful friendship. For the first time since Jennifer's death, Justin's smile was real.

33

Ian and Fiona

Having accepted the invitation to be the keynote speaker at the child protection conference, Fiona thought long and hard about what she wanted to talk about. It was a rare opportunity to get information to a large group of social workers, and she didn't want to mess it up. As usual, when faced with a decision that wasn't easy, she consulted Ian. They decided to take advantage of their experiences with the child protection system. They discussed the possibility of Fiona giving a talk on fostering children, or on abused children, or on parenting challenges. Noticing a distinct lack of enthusiasm for any of these, Ian had an idea.

"What about taking what happened to Heather as your starting point?"

"That's it. That's what I want to do. I'll talk about child sexual exploitation. It'll be difficult but I think I can make it powerful. Perfect."

The conference organizers had asked her to take an hour for her presentation. She was enthusiastic, though nervous about her ability to remain engaging for so long. But once she started working on her speech, she realized she had a lot to say. She started making notes on all the points she wished to cover.

As she did, she remembered a conversation with Justin one evening, when he had asked her whether children's rights were being respected in her profession. She had been embarrassed to admit she had never heard anything about children's rights. She was as surprised as Justin's students had been to hear children had rights separate from those of their parents. Having learned from Justin that they did, she was astonished that she had not learned about that in her years at university. She assumed that if she knew nothing about children having rights, it was likely that those in the audience wouldn't either. She decided to start the preparation for her speech by researching children's rights and seeing if they had any relevance to child protection. Justin had not provided any details.

Typing "children's rights" into Google search led Fiona to many sites about the United Nations Convention on the Rights of the Child. She quickly learned that it did indeed address sexual exploitation. She decided to start her talk with a slide of the text of article 34. It said that children have a right to be protected from all forms of sexual abuse and exploitation. That, she was pleased to learn, included child pornography, child prostitution, and sex-related trafficking. She would start with that, and she would end with the story of Heather. Now, how to fill in the rest? She would need to find a way to keep her audience interested throughout, which she realized, might not be a simple task.

"Ian, I have no idea how I'm going to talk for an hour without boring people to death. Can you help? You've given so many talks, you must have some tips on how to keep the audience interested."

"You know what I'd do, Fiona," Ian replied, "I'd use real life examples of children who've been sexually abused. Tell stories, the way I tell stories about Jesus."

They discussed this approach, and between them they came up with the idea of having a series of quotes from, or examples of, children who had experienced some form of sexual exploitation. While she displayed the quotes on the screen, she would address the whys, hows, and whats of each, and she would summarize the implications for social workers. She was excited to begin, and so back to Google search. She was astonished at how many stories of sexually exploited children there were on the internet. And they were from all parts of the world. The task she had set herself would not be easy, but if her talk could in any way contribute to stopping even one more child from being hurt like Heather, it would be worth it. Ian agreed.

Given the number of stories, Ian and Fiona decided they would each search the web to select out the cases they thought would hold the attention of the audience. They would then select from those the ones that reflected the different toxic effects on children. They had been looking less than five minutes when Ian came across a case that astonished him in its similarities to what happened to Heather. He called Fiona.

Together they read the case of an eleven-year-old who had used video chat to make new friends after her family moved. Fiona wondered if it was possible that kids that young would understand the risk of doing that. She felt sure that most kids would assume that they were chatting with someone around their own age. They wouldn't be expecting to be making friends with a pedophile posing as a peer. This girl obviously hadn't. She'd thought she was making friends with a teenage boy. She had no idea that she was being manipulated by a pedophile. As Fiona and Ian read on, they were appalled at the similarities to Heather's experience with Alexander. Like Heather, this girl had agreed to show her new friend her breasts.

"Maybe she needed the attention," Fiona commented. "But, Ian, this story shows how vulnerable children are to being groomed by pedophiles not just in person like Heather, but also online. This could easily happen to any child, even one in a stable and loving family."

They continued reading. The girl didn't know, the article said, that the guy was using screen capture. Predictably, he then threatened that if she did not agree to further sexual activity, he would make the images of her widely available.

"Oh Ian, I can't believe how much like our Heather's this girl's story is." She read on. The girl refused, and so he posted the images of her and made sure they were available to her friends on social media. The cyberbullying began immediately, and it never stopped.

"And just like Heather, this girl was horribly bullied at school. Why are kids so mean?" Ian asked Fiona, "and where were the teachers?"

Fiona sighed in response.

"The one difference is that this girl committed suicide. I guess, in a way, so did Heather."

They found many such stories and statistics. There were,

they discovered, millions of online photos of children being sexually abused. Some of the children were as young as three.

"Enough," said Fiona, with tears streaming down her cheeks. "I can't take any more right now."

"Are you sure you want to go ahead with this talk?" Ian asked, as he put his arms around her.

"I have to," she replied, "I have to. I hate it, but I have to. More than ever, I have to. But I just can't deal with anymore right now. Now I need to pray for peace and acceptance, but also for all the children. Let's just check that ours are all asleep and have an early night."

Fiona and Ian spent more time than usual looking at their peacefully sleeping children before they felt calm enough to go to bed themselves.

"I am having trouble feeling forgiveness," Ian commented, before he fell asleep.

34

Nigel and Malcolm

May fifth finally came. Nigel could hardly control his excitement as Quentin dropped him off at Heathrow in time for his flight to New York. A little over eight hours after takeoff, a very animated Nigel landed at JFK airport in New York. La Guardia would have been much closer but there was no direct flight. Malcolm had offered to pick Nigel up, but Nigel insisted he take a cab, given the distance. Nigel's first experience with a New York cabbie fit the stereotype. He was grateful to arrive safely at Malcolm's apartment in midtown Manhattan about an hour and a half after leaving the airport.

Nigel's first two weeks with Malcolm in New York passed quickly and blissfully. They spent their days sightseeing, and their nights having sex. Nigel was enthralled with the artwork at the Metropolitan Museum and the Museum of Modern Art but was overwhelmed with his discovery at the Morgan Library and Museum. There he found an amazing collection of music manuscripts, including works from Mozart, Verdi, and his beloved Puccini. His other highlight was the architecture of the Guggenheim. He was delighted to discover that it was a designated UNESCO World Heritage Site.

During this time, Malcolm and Nigel did not discuss

Samantha. They had a tacit agreement that they would not spoil their magical first weeks of being together with negativity. But it was always in Nigel's consciousness that he had a job to do in New York. It was neither an easy one, nor a pleasant one.

Exhaustion eventually set in. An excess of intellectual stimulation, and perhaps an excess of sex in place of sleep, caught up with them both. They took a few days to chill out. They took a break from the galleries and museums and limited their daily excursions to walks in the park. During their walks, Nigel thought long and hard about what he had agreed to do. He decided he could not go through with it. He was simply too happy. But Malcolm was not pleased when Nigel told him his decision.

"It's not that I am really keen on you killing her," he explained, "but I feel very strongly about commitment. You committed to a particular course of action, and now you say you have changed your mind. What am I to think? You also say you are committed to me, but does this mean you might change your mind about me too? Does commitment mean anything to you, Nigel?"

Nigel was stunned. Before he could reply, Malcolm strode ahead. Later, after they both calmed down, enjoyed a couple of glasses of wine, and Nigel had stressed how much he loved and wanted to be with Malcolm forever, they agreed to leave the subject alone for a few days and then talk it over. Three days later, they were tired of their self-imposed park walks, and ready for stimulation. They were also frustrated with the ongoing tension between them, and ready for distraction.

They went to the Museum of Natural History. Nigel was fine until he saw the Tyrannosaurus Rex. As he stood beside the fossil, grief for Harrison overcame him. His boy would have been ecstatic on seeing this magnificent skeletal creature. Nigel's eyes filled with tears and he let out a sob. Malcolm realized right away what Nigel was thinking. He put his arm around Nigel and led him out onto Central Park West.

As they emerged, they heard a squeal of brakes and saw a sports car skidding to a stop at a crosswalk on which three small children and a woman with a baby in a buggy were crossing.

"Oh my God," Malcolm gasped. "I'm sure that was Samantha driving. I recognized her from all the publicity shots and paparazzi photos. With that crazy red topknot, she's hard to miss. There she goes again. She almost killed another family."

Nigel was white and shaking. "Let's go back to your apartment and figure out how I'm going to put an end to this fucking bitch."

Malcolm's frustration with Nigel faded as he observed just how upset Nigel was. First was the memory of Harrison, and shortly after that, the witnessing of Samantha almost kill again. "Come on, time to go home." Malcolm kept his arm around a shaking Nigel as they walked back to the apartment.

"I have to do it now," Nigel said, still shaky. "She has to be stopped. Soon. My God, she could have killed those three little kids, or the baby or... what shall I do, how shall I stop her? I've got less than a week left here. Will you help me, Malcolm?"

"If you are absolutely sure and you are not going to change your mind again. We can talk it through. It's not going to be that easy here."

"Why not? I heard that it's easy to get guns in the US, and that you can just go buy one almost anywhere."

Malcolm chuckled. "Not anymore. It's true that most murders in the US are done with handguns, but it's not that easy to buy a gun in New York. I don't have one, and don't know anyone who does. I've never been interested in hunting or killing anyone—well not before I got entangled with you and that crazy gang in Phuket. But after what we saw today, I fully agree with you, we do need to act now."

"Do you think using a gun is our best hope?"

After discussing the various means of homicide, Nigel and Malcolm decided that shooting Samantha was likely the best method. But they needed to find a way that would not implicate either of them. They could not buy a gun legally. Nigel couldn't because he was not an American citizen. Malcolm wouldn't because he would need a background check, a permit, and an interview before being allowed to buy a gun. He was too concerned with being identified as the killer, assuming they were successful. What would he say was the purpose of buying a gun in his interview? The truth certainly wouldn't be a good idea, and why would an aspiring musician and opera star need a gun? After all, this was New York State. It had one of the lowest rates of handgun death in the country. If he lived somewhere like Maryland or Alaska, he could probably get away with the old argument of self-protection, but not in New York.

If they were to use a gun, they determined, they would have to get one on the black market. Neither knew how to go about this, but Malcolm had read once that most guns used to commit crimes in the city were from other states, and that gun traffickers were around who would sell to anyone.

Nigel was feeling an increasing level of despair. It did not seem possible that two guys who knew nothing about guns or killing could buy one that they would be able to use.

"It's not just getting a gun. We have to get the right ammo, load the damn thing it, and know how to use it. And of course, we can't be caught." Malcolm sounded frustrated.

"If our lives were a novel," Nigel said, "the right one would somehow fall into our hands. But this is reality and fate rarely works that way."

Malcom tried to lighten the mood. "Rarely is not never."

To relieve the tension, they went to a concert that evening. It was a warm starlit night, and so they walked the five kilometres to the concert. The hour's walk, followed by two hours of baroque music, calmed them.

They left feeling much better. It was still warm out so even though it was very late, they walked home. There were few people around as they walked hand in hand through different neighbourhoods. It was two in the morning as they came across a bar that was still serving.

"Let's stop for a nightcap, Nigel," said Malcolm. "We've been walking for ages and I could use a break."

The bar was busy, but they found an empty table in a corner. Malcolm ordered two Manhattans. "What?" said Nigel

"Is that really a drink?" The server laughed and winked at Malcolm.

"You'll love it. It's the perfect nightcap." The drinks came quickly.

Nigel tasted it. "I say Malcolm, it's great, but I have no idea what's in it, other than that's some sort of cherry on top, isn't it?"

Malcolm listed the ingredients he recalled were in the Manhattan: whisky, vermouth, and bitters. Nigel enjoyed it so much he wanted another.

After the second drink, Nigel was ready to leave. It was getting closer to three. First, he needed to use the washroom. He left Malcolm settling the tab and went to the men's room. It was small with only two urinals and each was in use, so Nigel went into one of the two stalls. As he relieved himself, he noticed something metallic behind the toilet tank, darker than the piping. When he looked closer and saw what it was, he could not believe his eyes and wondered if it was an illusion caused by exhaustion and too much alcohol. But it was real. Nigel un-taped a handgun from the back of the tank, slid it into the waistband of his chinos, and left the washroom.

"Quick Malcolm, we have to leave, now!" Back on the street he spoke in hushed tones of his find as they walked briskly away from the bar.

To his surprise, and somewhat horror, Nigel discovered when they got back that the gun had an indicator noting that it was loaded. This was all too much to take in. He fell into bed and slept soundly for six hours. When he awoke the next morning, he fully expected that the whole gun-finding incident had been a dream, but there it was in his suitcase where he had put it when they returned the previous night. Discussing their find over breakfast, Malcolm and Nigel agreed it was a sign of some sort of fate, although they could not explain what or how.

"Were this an opera," Malcolm commented, "there would be a musical motif now to signal the hand of fate." He started to sing.

"Stop joking around Malcolm. We need to decide where and how to use this thing fate has bestowed upon us, on our target."

Malcolm recalled reading that Samantha always attended the first matinee of each opera at the Met. She had Center Parterre Premium seating courtesy of her father who was a donor. Of course, Malcolm thought, Daddy would provide the best. He checked the schedule online and found that the first matinee performance of *Tosca* was that Saturday. That gave them three days to finish planning.

35

Alison and Simon

Simon and Alison looked forward to soon seeing Michael, Amy, and the grandchildren. Zachary had just turned sixteen, and Zoe was now fourteen. It seemed like a long time since they had spent any time with them, although virtual contact had been frequent.

The night before their flight to London, Alison suggested they eat out. She had cleaned out the fridge, and everything for the trip was packed. Simon, whose daily chore was to do the dinner dishes, readily agreed. They went to their favourite restaurant.

"Last time we were here," Alison said, as they were shown to a table, "we decided to go to Thailand. We already have a trip planned, so we don't need to make any decisions tonight."

"Not so sure about that." replied Simon "There actually is something I have been thinking about since Thailand. It's a pretty major decision."

Alison looked concerned. "What now?" she asked.

"Hear me out before you say anything. I've been thinking that maybe we should take early retirement. Being in Thailand, I realized how nice it is to be free of daily obligations and daily stresses."

"What stresses?" Alison interrupted.

"So much for hearing me out. Oh well." Simon continued, "I have been finding teaching increasingly stressful. For one thing, I get really pissed off when students sit in class looking at their phones instead of paying attention. That seems to be happening more and more."

"I know what you mean," Alison interrupted again. "I was lecturing about child abuse one day when I noticed a student smiling at her laptop. Nothing I was saying should have evoked a smile. So, I walked over to her and found that she was watching a YouTube video. Not that they are all like that but keeping their attention does seem harder than it used to."

Simon sighed. "Let's order. Do you want your usual burger and Bellini?"

"What else?" They ordered.

"Was there something else bothering you?" Alison asked.

"Yes. All the constraints on what we say and how we address the students. We have to be so damn careful not to offend them."

"Remember Peter from the psychology department, Simon? Since he was giving a lecture on adolescent development, he talked about breast growth. You'd think he'd raped someone. A group of girls went to the Dean to complain."

"That's the sort of thing I mean. And you can't use his or her anymore. Apparently, they like to be addressed in gender neutral, or non-binary, or whatever they call it, terms. No more he and she, no more him and her, only ze, zir, hir, tem, ve and who knows what. How the hell am I supposed to re-member?"

Alison was laughing. "It's not that hard! Remember how you moan and groan whenever a student calls you Mr. Lee-land instead of Dr. Leeland. It's a different generation. You should understand that. Come on you old fuddy-duddy. Get off the soapbox and enjoy your drink."

"Okay. It's not the most pressing problem, agreed. But there's one more thing. I was thinking that it would be great for us to have time to co-write a book on the antecedents of murder. It would build on the work we've done on the back-grounds of killers and malevolent leaders. What I see is one where you write about family conditions that are correlated with filicide, parricide, and child and spousal abuse, and I write about political and societal conditions that lead to state sanctioned murder like genocides."

"Sounds interesting. Maybe we could also look at the an-tecedents of the rise of right-wing populism, and why people like your buddy Trump get elected. Or we could write about vengeance killings, or preventive murders, or maybe even per-sonal experience with homicide?"

"Get serious, Alison. Would you consider retiring, do you think?"

"I'll think about it. And we'd have to see if the university will allow it. We are still on sabbatical and contractually oblig-ated to teach for a year after."

"True," Simon said. "I thought of that, but I'd bet they'd love to get rid of our senior prof salaries and hire a couple of new grads. You know how many are happy to get even a sessional contract."

"I suppose. But for now, let's just relax and enjoy the rest of our meal, go home, and get some sleep. We have to get up super early in the morning. Did you order to cab to the airport, Simon?"

During the seven-hour flight from New York to London, Alison thought about the pros and cons of taking early retirement. The lure of free time to travel, to write, to enjoy long walks, and to spend time with the grandchildren was attractive. Their income would be reduced, but that seemed less important than what they would gain. By the time they were in their final descent, she had made up her mind. She told Simon she'd ask for retirement when they got back.

"Great." Simon was visibly pleased. "Now I can really enjoy being in London, and you know something else we might consider—if Trump gets re-elected, we could move here."

* * *

Michael and Amy had offered to have them stay in their home, but Simon and Alison chose to stay in a hotel in central London. It would be an easy ride on the tube to see Zach and Zoe, and they could maintain their privacy. They opted for the Hilton Tower Bridge. It was close to a tube station, and it was close to the hospital where Miranda had worked—just in case they decided to go ahead with the plan. Simon had also heard that it was within walking distance to The Clink. As the oldest and most notorious prison in England, it was now a museum that he wanted to visit.

"Why am I not surprised," said Alison, when Simon said that The Clink was number one on his list of places he wanted to see during the trip. He was particularly eager to see the torture devices, he explained. Alison was more interested in the Tate Gallery which was also within walking distance of the hotel. But first, Michael and Amy and the two teenagers.

The family get together was joyous. Zach and Zoe were delightful. They liked the Thai carvings and clothes from Phuket, and the NY Yankee Hats and T-shirts Alison had picked up for them at JFK. They were particularly thrilled with the iPad Pro tablets. Michael and Amy expressed some concern that the kids were being spoiled, but Simon and Alison insisted that was their right as grandparents. Amy gave them each a big hug. Michael said how thrilled he was to see his parents looking so healthy.

"You look like the Phuket holiday was a great success," he commented, hugging each of them. "You look great, and you're still tanned—it must be over two months since you left."

"Yes. It was remarkably interesting and has certainly had a lasting impression on us." Alison recalled the moments of fear as she packed ten castor bean seeds deep in her check-in luggage.

Back in their hotel much later that evening, Simon and Alison discussed the feasibility of finding Miranda, getting her to chew at least eight of the seeds, and whether they could in fact go through with the killing. Being in England made things seem vastly different from the easy discussions of murder over drinks in the lounge in Phuket.

"I wonder what channels we get on TV," Simon said, as he found the remote and turned the television on. Alison was getting ready for bed.

"Hey Alison, we get CNN."

"Mmm." Alison looked up at the ad, yawned, and crawled under the sheets.

36

Ian and Fiona

Lachlan, Caitlin, and Maggie were running endlessly around the kitchen table flapping their arms and shouting "We're gonna fly!" Ian and Fiona were not surprised by the children's excitement. They were leaving for Vancouver the following morning. The day was busy with last minute household chores and packing. The children had to be convinced that they would not need to take any toys other than games or books for the flight. Fiona had already packed the notes for her talk, and the thumb drive with the slide presentation. For the fifth time she checked her bag to make sure it had not somehow left while she was not watching it. Ian grinned.

"Do you have our tickets, Ian?" Fiona's anxiety was palpable.

"Gee, I wonder what I did with them."

Ian chuckled as Fiona looked aghast and asked, "Where are they Ian, quit kidding around."

"They are probably where I put them," he teased. "They rarely take off on their own."

The evening passed in a flurry of excitement and anxiety, and the night with little sleep. The cab arrived as scheduled at seven the following morning. One very happy and excited family went to the airport. Aside from almost losing Maggie, who ran off to pet a dog she saw near the baggage carousel, all went well. Prior to boarding, Fiona reminded the children how to behave on the flight. She had heard many stories from friends about being kicked in the back by a child behind them, or having to listen to children screaming, or having to dodge them running down the aisle to the washroom. She needn't have worried.

Once seated, all three were quiet. Lachlan was busy looking out the window, Caitlin was reading a book, and Maggie was enjoying the attention from the flight attendants. The ninety-minute flight to Toronto passed without incident and Fiona came close to relaxing. There was a two-hour layover at Pearson airport where they had lunch. The children were rarely allowed fast food, so they were thrilled to be allowed to have burgers and fries for lunch.

After the five-hour flight from Toronto to Vancouver, the children were tired and restless, and Maggie was whining. For the first time since they had decided to take the children to Vancouver, Fiona wondered if bringing the children had been the right choice. The cab ride into the city was long and slow, and Maggie was increasingly fussy. Lachlan told her to settle down; she responded by crying loudly. Ian decided he would have to give the driver an extra-large tip. What a start, he thought. Whatever possessed us to bring three kids across the country?

"Come on you three," Ian said, "we understand you're tired and that's okay, we've had a long day. But you need to quiet down so that the driver can get us to our hotel."

Fiona smiled at him, "We'll be there soon," she added, "and we'll all have something to eat and a rest."

Checking into the hotel, Fiona briefly noticed the glorious setting with the sparkling ocean and the mountains across from the hotel, but she was exhausted. After checking there was an extra cot in the room for Maggie, and enough space for everyone to sleep, Fiona unpacked what each of them would need for overnight. She then ordered sandwiches from room service which they ate before falling into bed and a deep sleep.

When they woke the next morning, Vancouver was living up to its stereotype. The city was pretty much fogged in, and rain fell relentlessly. Fortunately, Fiona had been proactive and checked indoor activities before they came.

"It's a Science World Day," she announced.

To Fiona's knowledge it was one of the few places to go on a rainy day in the city that had activities for children from toddlerhood to teenage, and she loved that it was run by a non-profit group. She also thought that both she and Ian would enjoy seeing the building. Neither of them had ever seen a geodesic dome before. They spent an enchanting day there. As promised, there were lots of hands-on activities for each of the children, a good cafeteria for lunch, and an excellent nature film in the OMNIMAX theatre at the very top of the building.

"You know, Ian," said Fiona, as they went back to the hotel. "I think this city is a great place for children. Why was I ever worried about bringing them here?"

* * *

"Wake up you guys," said Lachlan, as the three children jumped on their parents' bed the next morning. "It's sunny out and we want to go to the beach." It was the last day before the conference started. They had promised the children that if the weather was nice, they would go to Stanley Park and one of the beaches there. When they asked the concierge at the hotel which beach he recommended, he suggested they might first enjoy renting bicycles and riding around the seawall. Then they could see the different beaches and choose one.

"I think Maggie is too young for that," said Ian. "She's only four."

"No problem, you can get a bike with a kiddie seat on the back and strap her in that. It's good for kids under six so she'll be fine."

Ian asked the other children if they would like to do that. They were enthusiastic.

It was a longer ride than they anticipated. After forty minutes, Caitlin was complaining her legs were tired, so they took a break and stretched out on the grass. Maggie was delighted at the number of dogs she noticed who were being taken for walks around the seawall.

"Can we have a puppy when we get home?" she asked. Fortunately, she was easily distracted with the promise of seeing more animals along the seawall. The family cycled further along the seawall, with several short stops to admire views, sculptures, and memorials.

An hour and a half later, hungry and tired, they stopped at a large beach. They bought cold drinks, hotdogs, and chips from the cafeteria which they enjoyed at a picnic table. After eating, the children played on the beach. Fiona had brought along a copy of her talk, so she read over that. Ian watched the children playing and his wife studying and felt a deep contentment. He decided that family holidays were to be preferred over more exotic ones without the children. He said a silent prayer of thanks for all the blessings in his life. He fervently hoped the peace he felt would last.

37

Nigel and Malcolm

The opening day for *Tosca* came. The sublime music belied the dark action of the political thriller. Like so many operas, the story of *Tosca* ended with death, in this case, with an execution followed by a suicide. Nigel hoped this was not prophetic.

He'd had almost no sleep the night before. He came perilously close to changing his mind again. How, he wondered, had it come to this? He, a peace and nature loving man, had agreed to kill a human being, had a plan to do so, and a loaded gun at his bedside. He got up a few times and paced around the living room. He wondered if he should just leave. He could just get a cab to the airport and the first flight possible back to London. He'd had a terrific time with Malcolm, and he had been to all the places he had hoped to visit. The trip had been spectacular. Why ruin it with such a heinous act? But that would mean reneging on his commitment. And that would mean the end of his relationship with Malcolm. He could not do anything to jeopardize what they had together. Part of him was concerned that Malcolm had been so adamant that he proceed with this bizarre commitment. Why was that? Was Malcolm not what he seemed? But his love for Malcolm was stronger than any apprehensions. Malcolm is such a good person, he told himself, it must mean that he is worried that Samantha will kill again, or maybe he is pushing me into this so that Harrison's death will be avenged by Simon and Alison. Nigel tossed and turned.

What if I run, and then Samantha kills other pedestrians or a passenger, or child? She just might. He recalled seeing Samantha driving carelessly, the squeal of the brakes, the fear on the children's faces, the horror on their mother's. He recalled the story of Melody's life and tragic loss. He understood their pain too well. It was not a hurt he wished on anyone.

His exhaustion eventually overtook his anxiety, and he slept for three hours. Waking at six, he felt groggy, overwhelmed, and more nervous than he had ever been about anything in his life. But he was determined to go ahead. He had told Simon and Alison he would, and he had promised Malcolm that he would remain a man of his word. And he did believe that killing this particular one individual may well save five others. He had no choice.

Malcolm was aware of Nigel's tension and was feeling somewhat anxious himself. They distracted themselves as much as possible through the morning by going out for brunch. Neither had any appetite, although both appreciated the mimosas. Back at Malcolm's apartment, they reviewed the plan. They decided they would walk along Broadway to Lincoln Square. The walk should help alleviate the tension, and it would mean no record of them going there by cab or public transit. Anonymity would be essential. Once at the Lincoln

Center, they would mingle with the crowds as they emerged from the opera.

The time to leave came all too quickly. The day was cool for May. Nigel's overcoat did not look inappropriate. Although there would be thousands of people leaving at around the same time, they felt confident they would be able to spot Samantha. With her bright red hair and above average height, Samantha should be easy to see in a crowd. They also knew from which exit she would most likely emerge. There had recently been an article about her in a gossip column in which it was noted which zone she always sat in at the Met, along with which designer she most often wore, her favourite hairstylist, and who she was currently dating. The columnist, Gabby Greer, had also reported that Samantha always left the opera immediately and always went to the Empire Rooftop Bar for cocktails after. Malcolm was wryly amused that such trivia could help plan what he hoped and expected to be the perfect murder. Thanks GG, he said to himself.

* * *

The walk along Broadway was uneventful. Malcolm and Nigel arrived at the Lincoln Center a few minutes after four. "We have a good half hour to kill," Malcolm said.

Nigel was not amused. Malcolm suggested getting coffee, but Nigel said he was anxious enough and didn't think caffeine would be helpful. He felt for the gun which he had put in an inside pocket of his overcoat. It was still there.

"Let's sit here," Malcolm pointed to a table at an outdoor

café, "and have a soda 'til it's time. And please quit fiddling with the heat—it's making me nervous!"

"Okay. Make mine soda water please. I'll do my best to sit and behave. Nervous? Tell me about it."

Twenty minutes later, it was time to put their plan into action. They left the café and walked into the square. Standing shielded by Malcolm, Nigel moved the gun from his pocket to his right hand. The sleeves on his coat were long and loose enough that he could pretty much conceal the gun while holding the barrel in his hand. Walking slowly, side by side, they neared the general area where they expected to see Samantha as she exited. Nigel was close to hyperventilating at this point. Malcolm was also getting nervous while trying to calm Nigel. The doors opened.

Nigel scanned the emerging crowd. He realized he was hoping Samantha would not come out, or not be seen by them, or someone would see the gun and stop him, or … but there she was, exactly where they had predicted. She was unmistakable. It was, Nigel realized, too late to do anything but go ahead with the killing.

"There she is." Malcolm whispered to Nigel. "Let's roll."

They walked as casually as they could toward Samantha. There was a throng of people around her as well as her date, a young man who did not seem to be paying any attention to her as they left.

The noise of the crowd mixed with the noise of the city—the inescapable wailing sirens, the heavy traffic, car horns, trucks rumbling, people shouting, children crying, dogs barking, and the hissing sound of the brakes on a bus.

Nigel heard nothing. He was totally focused on getting close enough to the target to do what he must. He had shifted to thinking only of doing the job well. Keeping his eyes on her, and with Malcolm walking alongside, he came closer and closer to Samantha. Nigel planned to be within inches of her before pulling the trigger.

"Another three feet," whispered Malcolm. Nigel nodded; his mouth was too dry to speak.

Suddenly there was a very loud pop like a firework exploding. The noise startled Malcolm. Was it possible that Nigel had used the gun without him noticing? Had it discharged by accident? But Nigel was standing beside him looking even more stunned than Malcolm was feeling. Less than three feet away, Samantha lay bleeding. Someone pushed in front of them. The crowd moved on. Nigel and Malcolm allowed themselves to be swept up by the seemingly oblivious crowd. They left the square. More sirens sounded.

They walked home along the East River, not talking, but holding hands. Along the way, something fell out of Nigel's other hand, hit the water with a loud plop, and disappeared. A little further along, Nigel slipped out of his coat, and dropped it in the water. Neither felt like eating dinner. It was around seven when Malcolm turned the television on.

"This just in." Wolf Blitzer was reporting on CNN. "Well-known socialite and heiress Samantha Costner was shot to death this afternoon outside the Met opera. Police report being appalled that no one stopped to help her as she lay bleeding in Lincoln Square. She was pronounced dead at the scene.

There is no suspect at this time. More news as it comes available."

38

Alison and Simon

Simon and Alison were in their hotel room in London watching CNN's international news. "*Breaking News. Heiress shot and killed leaving Met opera. Persons of Interest being sought.*" The line going across the bottom of the screen was unmistakable. Bianca Nobilo reported that police in New York were searching for a couple they wished to talk to regarding the shooting death of well-known American heiress and socialite, Samantha Costner. Although they had no suspects or eyewitnesses at this time, she reported, there were several people who may have had the motive to end Samantha's life. Bianca went on to describe Samantha and what was known about her, but Alison and Simon did not hear it. Alison was sitting up in bed white-faced, and Simon was pacing the length of the room.

"It's us they are looking for, right?" she asked. "But our alibi is airtight. We're here. We weren't in New York. There'll be a record of us on the flight and in this hotel."

"Yup, oh my God, Alison. Nigel did it. You realize what that means. We have no choice now but to go ahead with Miranda. He did it. I can't believe it. Nigel actually did it. It's not a game anymore. Revenge for Melody and all the others she's killed, and those whose lives she's ruined."

"But you know Simon, I realize now that even as I packed the seeds, I never really intended to kill Miranda. Oh God. What'll we do?"

"Maybe it's just a coincidence—maybe someone else shot her," Simon suggested.

"As if, as Zoe would say."

Simon and Alison were restless all day. Neither slept much that night. They had arranged to see the grandchildren the next day and agreed that the distraction would be good for them. It would also allow them to delay making any decisions about Miranda. They took Zach and Zoe on a three-hour cruise down the Thames to Hampton Court Palace. Nigel had recommended they go to the maze if they were ever in the area. According to the *Guinness World Records*, it was the oldest hedge maze in the world.

The cruise was relaxing, and they enjoyed getting lost in the maze. For a few hours at least, their minds were occupied with the present. But at the end of the day, after they had seen Zoe and Zach home, their thoughts returned to Miranda and what they had committed to do. They discussed their options after dinner that evening and decided that they would take it a step at a time and see how things played out.

Step one was to see if they could find where Miranda lived or hung out. If they couldn't, then they couldn't be faulted for not carrying through their end of the bargain. But they did. It took fewer than five minutes to find her on the internet. There were photos of her standing outside her flat, and although the street number was not given, the neighbourhood was.

"Too bad," said Alison, "maybe we should just go for a walk around there tomorrow."

"Okay, and if there are no pubs or cafes around, then we will have no way of getting to her, right?"

"Right," answered Alison. "I really need to get some sleep tonight. You know the other thing we should do tomorrow," she yawned, "is get in touch with the NYPD and tell them we just heard and give them our flight numbers, so they'll know it wasn't us."

"You're right as always, Mrs. Leeland. Good night my darling, and let's hope we sleep."

After walking in Miranda's neighbourhood the next day, Simon and Alison were increasingly anxious. It had been all too easy to spot the building she lived in, and to make matters worse, there was an attractive looking pub on the street corner. They went into the pub hoping it would be full of old men playing darts, but it was full of young adults and there was no dart board in sight.

"Another stereotype shattered," said Simon.

"And step two is leading us closer to the criss-cross target. But maybe she doesn't hang out there."

That evening they went to the pub, sat at the bar and ordered a beer. It was warm.

"Ugh," said Simon, "one stereotype supported."

A young woman came in and sat at the bar a few stools down from Alison.

"Evening Miranda. The usual, my love?" asked the bartender. At least three other patrons greeted her by name also. It was obvious she was a regular. The bartender pushed a drink in her direction as soon as she sat down, and then gave her a bowl of munchies. Alison watched with interest and a growing sense of excitement.

"Finish your beer, Simon, and let's get out of here. I have an idea and I need to talk to you."

As they walked back to their hotel, they agreed she was definitely the right Miranda. Everything fit with what Nigel had told them. Alison shared her idea. She had watched Miranda taking handfuls of the nuts and pretzels from the bowl without looking at them. She munched them and washed them down hastily. Alison wondered, she told Simon, if they could sneak the ricin seeds into the bowl of snacks.

"But what do they taste like?" he asked.

"Good question. I have no idea. It's not likely she'd eat enough if they were disgusting, even if we could sneak them in. But if she didn't eat them, we'd have done our part without actually killing her. Let's search on Google when we get back."

For once, Google was not helpful. Every page that purported to explain the taste of castor beans came up either with a not available or a removed message. If they were going to go ahead, they would have to take a chance. Both hoped the taste was so vile, Miranda would not actually eat them. They decided they would go back to the pub a few times to see if what they had observed was typical and if it was, then they would take the seeds and see if there was a way of sneaking them into the bowl of munchies.

The rest of the week passed with delightful and relaxing days spent sightseeing with Zach, Zoe, Michael, and Amy. The evenings, when they would go to the pub for what they had come to think of as their daily scouting report, were increasingly tense. They took the weekend to spend entirely with the family.

At the beginning of the next week, their last in England, it was back to the pub. Miranda's bar stool sat empty. Simon, who'd had several friendly chats with the bartender, pointed to the empty seat and commented, "Your cute young regular's not here tonight."

"That was a tragic one, guv," he said, sighing. "She was here Saturday night with her boyfriend Jimmie. They'd often come in together for a few before they went out on the town. As usual, they had a few drinks. Then they got into a bit of an argument, dunno what it was about, but Jimmie looked right pissed and he left. Then she went to the loo. She never came out. Mrs. Jones found her there. Word is she overdosed."

"That's awful," Simon said, looking disbelieving. "Was she known to use drugs?"

"Yes, 'fraid so. Nice enough kid, but we all knew she and Jimmie were heroin junkies. Didn't used to be so bad, but there've been problems with fentanyl around here. Probably some in their smack. Likely she ended up having some sort of allergic reaction to the combo of the booze and heroin laced with fentanyl. I've heard of that before. Whatever it was, it sure killed her quickly. One more dumb dead kid. Tragic how they keep doing it to themselves."

Ian and Fiona

The day of Fiona's presentation started early. She was out of the shower while the children were still in pajamas watching cartoons on TV: a vacation treat. Ian would take them to Stanley Park after breakfast. Fiona needed to be at the registration desk in the ballroom before nine. Her talk was scheduled to start at ten. With the time the conference organizers allowed for questions, she would be on the stage until at least eleven-thirty. Lunch was being served between noon and one.

She became increasingly nervous as delegates entered the vast room where the podium and mic were set up for her. She checked that her slide presentation was working, and that there was a glass of water at the podium. By the time she was introduced, the room was full. She took a deep breath, reminded herself that she was telling the listeners a story they needed to hear, and began.

Once she started to speak, she relaxed, and even more so as she noticed the attentive faces among her audience. People were nodding as she stated key points. The room became quiet as she related tragic incidents of child sexual exploitation. She remembered Ian's advice to give people a chance to absorb information, and she paced herself by taking sips of water. This is going well, she thought.

In the meantime, Ian and the children planned to go back to the park. This time they would walk around Lost Lagoon and then go to the playground. He picked up some juice boxes, fruit, and sandwiches at a small convenience store a block from the hotel, and put them in his backpack along with tissues, Band-Aids, and sunscreen. We're set for the day, and ready for anything, he thought. It was a short walk from the hotel to Lost Lagoon, but Ian carried Maggie on his shoulders so that she would not get tired before they got there.

They all enjoyed their walk around the lagoon. The children were enchanted with all the ducks, herons, and swans they saw on the water and in the reeds. But the highlight was when a mother raccoon with five kits emerged from the undergrowth. Ian was momentarily afraid she might attack the children, but she simply sauntered by followed by the five little mini-me's, as Ian thought of them.

"I want one of those," Maggie announced, pointing at a kit. The others laughed. They stopped at the Nature House where Ian bought some postcards, and some books for the children to read on the plane ride home. It was an idyllic morning. This is wonderful, he thought, and hoped Fiona's presentation was going well.

Ian and the children ate their lunch on a picnic table that was between the washrooms and the playground by Second Beach. After lunch, Caitlin took Maggie into the women's washroom while Lachlan used the men's. Ian stood between both washrooms, eyeing anyone else that entered, and ready to dash in to either one if the children called for him. When they came out, the children were eager to go play on the equipment. Ian asked them to wait at the table while he went to the washroom, but they cajoled him, and he finally agreed on the condition that the two older children watch Maggie closely until he returned. After all, he thought, I will be less than five minutes.

The children happily ran off together toward the swings. Four minutes later, Ian emerged and looked down at the play area. He spotted Caitlin and Lachlan right away. But where was Maggie? He looked at each group of children, at families sitting around with their dogs. He could not see Maggie. He ran over to the other children. "Where's Maggie?"

"She's here, dad," said Lachlan, "on the swing." But she wasn't. Maggie was gone.

Ian was frantic. Telling Caitlin and Lachlan to stand by the picnic table and not move, he ran down toward the beach. Maybe Maggie had gone to play in the sand. Calling her name over and over, he searched the beach area. No Maggie. He ran back to the playground.

"Maggie!" he called out. "Maggie, where are you?"

He asked the children on the swings "Did any of you see a little girl around here? She was wearing red shorts and a white T-shirt with a puppy picture on it."

"She went with her dad and their puppy over there," said one of the children, pointing to the tunnel that was the walking route between the playground and Lost Lagoon.

Ian blanched and instinctively started praying as he ran through the tunnel calling Maggie's name. It reverberated.

"Maggie, Maggie, Maggie." He felt like the tunnel was mocking him. Reaching the other side, he saw only ducks.

Ian's panic intensified. His heartbeat was fast and loud. He was sweating. He felt like vomiting. Was it really possible that someone had taken his Maggie? It can't be, he thought. This must be a nightmare. I'll wake up soon and tell Fiona. But it was real. He heard a noise coming from a path that led away from the lagoon into the woods. He could not identify it but thought it could be the sound of his Maggie crying.

The path was narrow and uneven, with many tree roots across it, and it was dark from the shade of the tall trees all around. The forest was becoming thicker. The path thinned, and branches blocked the way. Ian tripped over a tree root as he tried to speed up. He got up, wincing in pain from his ankle. He picked up a thick stick to help push branches aside and continued as quickly as he could. Hearing a rustling noise, he stopped and looked around. Only trees and more trees.

"Maggie, is that you?" he called. But as he looked around him, he saw that it was a squirrel. Was the squirrel trying to tell him something with its chattering and tail jerking? Please God, send a sign, he begged silently. Am I on the right track? What if Maggie is somewhere else? The squirrel hopped onto a branch closer to Ian and chirped again. Ian started hyperventilating. Calm down, he told himself. He checked his watch. It had been only ten minutes since he went to the washroom. It felt like an eternity. Dear God, he pleaded silently, let me find Maggie safe and sound. I'll spend my life in your service, I promise to only do what is right and holy, please God, I must find Maggie.

The path narrowed even more and then faded into multiple possible trails. Overhead, a bald eagle flew making its characteristic weirdly weak and high-pitched squeak. He called again, as loudly as he could. "Maggie, Maggie are you there? Maggie I am coming. Maggie, do you hear me?"

The eagle squeaked again. Was it trying to guide him, he wondered. Is this a sign from God or have I gone mad? He ran on as best he could. His chest hurt. His knees hurt. His feet hurt. Most of all his heart hurt. He briefly thought of the other children, waiting by the swings. He briefly thought of Fiona, at her conference expecting an evening with the family. God, he thought, why hast thou forsaken me? This thought was quickly followed by a feeling of guilt. How could he be talking like he was Jesus? But he was feeling abandoned by God. But maybe God was speaking to him through the eagle. "Maggie," he called, "Maggie!" He heard a noise just ahead of him. He stopped and listened. "Maggie," he called again, "is that you?" He heard something again. He could not identify the sound.

* * *

Fiona was elated. She was overwhelmed by the standing ovation her talk received and was even more pleased by the comments and questions that she received over lunch. She had hoped that she would make a difference. Judging by the comments, especially those about Heather, she knew she had been successful. Happy and relaxed, Fiona went to the afternoon session she had registered for. It was a round table discussion on cyber bullying. After that, she would have time to freshen up before the family got back to the hotel.

She was really looking forward to the evening. She had booked a table at the Old Spaghetti Factory in Gastown as a surprise for Ian and the children. She looked forward to their happy reaction when she told them, and especially when they arrived. She had convinced the staff to reserve them a table in the old streetcar. The children would be thrilled. She was feeling content as she went into the elevator and up to their room.

When the family arrived back at the hotel, all plans of a celebratory dinner at the Old Spaghetti Factory were gone in an instant. Caitlin and Lachlan were unusually quiet and subdued. They were uninterested in going out for dinner, wanting only to pack and go home. Ian was a mess, physically and emotionally. He had cuts and scrapes on his arms and face, and his clothes had vomit splattered all over them. He was agitated and clearly distressed.

Maggie was in the worst state of them all. Her face was smeared with tears, her eyes red, her mouth looked swollen, and she smelled odd. Fiona could not identify the smell other than to think of it as part vomit, part chemical. No one could, or would, tell her what had happened. The older children said they didn't know what happened except that Maggie had been sick. Ian said only "God forgive me."

The MOE Gang

The headlines in newspapers and online were the same.

Stanley Park Body Identified

The badly decomposed body found in Vancouver's Stanley Park five weeks ago has now been identified as that of fifty-four-year-old Blake Phillips of Quesnel, British Columbia. The autopsy revealed that the cause of death was homicide, not the result of a bear attack as some sources had originally reported. According to a source familiar with the autopsy, there was extensive damage to the bones of the face and the skull consistent with a violent attack with an object such as a jagged rock.

Phillips, who had a history of child sexual assault convictions, was well-known to police in the Cariboo region. Local police were not aware of Phillips presence in Vancouver. Reports are that he was there in violation of a parole order to not leave Quesnel. Police have no suspects at this time. Anyone with any information is asked to contact the Vancouver Police or their local RCMP office.

Nigel was enjoying a nightcap in his study when he saw the bulletin on a CNN international news round up. The news anchor noted that when the body was first found, it was described as one of the grisliest discoveries ever made by a hiker.

He then called in an expert who affirmed that the autopsy indicated extensive anger on the part of the killer.

"I have never seen such a true crime of passion," Dr. Boghosian said. "Whoever did this was fuelled by uncontrollable rage. When a person is very angry," he explained, "the body automatically secretes adrenaline, which is the hormone that prepares you to do battle. You feel empowered and strong. You know the Roman philosopher Seneca went as far as to describe anger as a 'short madness' that sets us on the path to self-destruction."

A panel of experts in homicide followed Dr. Boghosian, and they agreed it was likely a parent of one of the children Phillips had abused. That would account for the rage. But each had been thoroughly investigated, they reported, and each had an airtight alibi.

Nigel was stunned. He called Malcolm from the garden to tell him. "It's not like when we read about Miranda's overdose death, is it, Malcolm," Nigel said. "We knew that Simon and Alison were in the city. Not sure how they got away with it, but the way the media reported it as the hundredth teenager to die of a drug overdose in the past three months put all the attention on Miranda's behaviour. Seems like no one ever thought of any other possibility."

"But this couldn't possibly have been the Rev," Malcolm replied. "He was the most adamant of the group that killing was always wrong. Anyway, he lived on the other side of the country. Just a weird coincidence."

Nigel and Malcolm had settled in London. Believing Simon and Alison to have killed Miranda, and assuming that they would think Nigel had murdered Samantha, they never wanted to see them again. They wanted nothing more to do with guns, or violence, or murderers. London, at least Nigel's version of it, provided the city lifestyle they wanted without all the violence. Malcolm loved the peacefulness and beauty of Nigel's estate. He was enchanted with the history of London and could not believe his good fortune when he successfully auditioned for a role at the Royal Opera House. No more New York and no more Phuket. By next January, Nigel's book would be released, and Malcolm would be singing his dream role of Rodolfo. Life was better than either of them had thought possible.

* * *

Simon was surfing through online news when he saw the report. He called Alison into his study and showed her the article on his tablet. They realized immediately who Blake was. Just as quickly, they decided with some relief that it could not have been Ian or Fiona who was responsible. Of all the group, it was Fiona and the Rev who were the most unwavering in their belief that there could no circumstances under which killing was acceptable. It was unthinkable that either of them could be violent.

"Coincidence," Simon concluded.

"Or karma," said Alison. "But between this death, Samantha's murder, and Miranda's overdose, I really regret ever introducing the trolley problem to the group."

"It's not your fault Ali." Simon put his arm around her and squeezed gently. "Let it go."

Back home in New York, he and Alison were resting after shopping for Michael's upcoming visit. They had agreed that they wanted to keep in closer contact and be a more meaningful part of the grandchildren's lives. What they decided was feasible was one trip a year. Either they would go to London, or the family would come to New York. Despite his parents having just been in London, Michael had made an exception and told them he would visit them in New York soon. He had told them that they seemed distracted when in London and he wanted to ensure they were okay. They assured him they were just nervous about starting their retirement.

After this trip, they could connect with Skype or Zoom. They were also planning to invite both Zach and Zoe to spend next summer with them, without their parents. There were so many events and places to enjoy with the grandchildren before they got any older. Now that they were retired, family, they had decided, was the most important thing in life. They had missed too many years of their grandchildren's lives. Family, Simon had avowed, should never be taken for granted.

* * *

Justin connected to the Wi-Fi in his aunt's apartment and checked the Canada news on his phone. He had arrived in Thailand earlier in the day and was staying with his aunt until he found a place to rent. His teaching job, just south of Bangkok, started in five weeks. As he read the news item about Jennifer's uncle, his body tensed. He felt hot and sick. The image of Jennifer last time he had seen her was vivid. He put down his phone and went out into the crowds to walk.

He wondered who had killed Jennifer's uncle. The one thing he was sure of was that it could not have been Ian. The others might have carried out their horrible criss-cross plans, but not the Rev and Fiona. He had heard about Samantha's murder and now Blake. He didn't know about Miranda, but he hoped Alexander would never be killed. He would hate to think the others would assume he was responsible. No, he thought, it wasn't Fiona or the Rev. Of that, he was sure. But who and why?

He forced his thoughts to the future. In a few days, Elaine was flying over from Korea where she had a new teaching position. She had previously been in Samut Prakan, where Justin would teach, and she agreed to show him around and help him find a place. Justin was looking forward to exploring the Ancient City. He had read that it was known as the world's largest museum, and he was interested in seeing some of the ancient religious objects in the Erawan Museum. Mostly, he was looking forward to seeing Elaine.

* * *

Fiona saw the news in *The Globe and Mail*, a Canadian national newspaper. Fortunately, she was sitting down when she saw it. In a state of disbelief, she read it twice. She vaguely remembered seeing the initial reports of a hiker coming across a body in the park, but she had not given it any thought at the time. This was different. She felt like her blood was turning to ice and she started to feel dizzy. She did not like what she was thinking. She had never understood what happened that last day in Vancouver. The day had gone so well until Ian and the children came back from the park.

She read the item again. With hands shaking so badly she could barely type, she searched the web looking for more information. What she found strongly suggested that Blake was probably killed at the time they were in Vancouver. It had happened in Stanley Park where Ian had taken the children. And, she realized to her horror, this Blake was Jennifer's uncle; a man who abused children. Too much of a coincidence, she wondered. It would explain the state of the family that day, Maggie's regressive behaviours, and Ian's breakdown. But what was she thinking? Ian, her Ian, a vicious murderer? It could not be, she thought. But the pieces all fit. Was it possible? The doubt was excruciating. The certainty, she felt, more so.

Rebecca, March 2019-November 2020

It had been a long day. First, an eight-hour overnight flight squashed in economy with a child behind her kicking her seat, and now a one-hour train ride from Schiphol Airport to The Hague. Inspector Rebecca Youngman was exhausted. But she was looking forward to her first international conference on unsolved murders. And she was looking forward to four whole days free from the daily chaos of trying to be a good detective and single parent of a rambunctious two-year-old.

Glancing at her seatmate, she noticed he was reading the conference program. "Looks like you're going where I am."

"The murder conference," he said, grinning. "Hi, John MacDonald. I'm here from Halifax in Nova Scotia, hoping to get some ideas on how to bring closure to a cold case that's been bugging me for over a year now." They shook hands.

"Rebecca Youngman, from Manhattan. I've also been struggling with an unsolved murder. It was incredible. The most brazen yet successful I have ever heard of. Here's this crowd leaving the Met opera on a Saturday afternoon when this well-known woman is shot in the chest and no one saw a thing. Not even her toy boy date—some soap opera star, I think. He was probably too busy with his adoring fans to pay attention to her. She fell bleeding. Not a single witness. Unbelievable. The only clue we had is that we knew who would want this woman dead. But they all had airtight alibis." Rebecca yawned.

"I'll tell you my story later, you look beat. Go ahead and rest. I'll wake you when we get in and maybe we can share a cab to the hotel. Are you staying at the Kurhaus?"

"Of course, it looks like a fabulous spot for a conference, it's right across from the beach." Yawning again, Rebecca closed her eyes.

When the cab, which they had taken from the train station, pulled up outside the impressive exterior of the hotel, Rebecca wanted nothing more than to sleep. To her dismay, check-in time was three hours later. Sitting with John drinking coffee, she realized that many of the other red-eyed coffee drinkers around them were also there for the conference. They were all looking through the conference materials. This should be good, she thought, relaxing. There would only be twenty in attendance, and she knew from the speakers' program that most were seasoned veterans. What she was most looking forward to was the workshop where she, John, and two others would be discussing their unsolved cases. According to the program, in addition to her and John there was a Chris Andris from Vancouver, and a Casey Remington from London. She desperately wanted to go home with some new ways of identifying the brazen Met shooter as some of the media had called him or her. At the very least, she hoped to enjoy a few long walks on the beach across from the hotel.

* * *

The conference did not turn out the way Rebecca expected. She had learned nothing that would help her find the perp in the Met Murder, and it had rained every day. But she had quickly developed a friendship with John. Flying back to New York, Rebecca remembered the overwhelming pessimism and depression that had become part of her job. A month later she had left the police force and was working as private security guard. She stayed in touch with John.

A year later, Rebecca was living with John in Nova Scotia. They were the owner-operators of the South Shore Inn, a small hotel on the Atlantic Ocean and a few kilometres south of Halifax. They both found the surf and seagulls more to their liking than the sleaze and slaughter they had dealt with daily as detectives. When the inn wasn't busy, they spent their time walking the beaches with Leah. It had not been busy for a while. Like much of the world, Nova Scotia had been affected by the COVID-19 pandemic. But unlike so many places, the case and death numbers in Nova Scotia had stayed low. Because of that, the inn could stay open throughout, but Rebecca and John had limited guests to locals only.

It was a Saturday afternoon on a perfect fall day. Rebecca and John were walking hand in hand along the water's edge while Leah ran ahead with Calypso, their rescue potcake dog.

"You know, John," Rebecca said, as she stopped to admire a piece of driftwood, "I was thinking back to when we first met. At the time, I was so upset that I didn't get what I needed from the conference. I hated myself, and I hated being a failure. There was a cold-blooded killer out there and it was my fault. What if he or she killed again? I was so stressed and angry all the time I found myself yelling at Leah for nothing. No kid should have to put up with a frustrated and angry mom."

"I know what you mean about the conference, Becca," John said. "When we were at the workshop with Chris and Casey, I thought we'd all go home and find our killers. But none of us did. Not even the perp of that brutal killing in Vancouver."

"If only murderers had some sort of sign on their foreheads, our job would have been easy. But, as we both know, anyone can be a killer. Your grandma could be a murderer, your banker, your teacher, your church minister, or even our guests. Who knows? But that's not our problem anymore. Let's just think about all the good times we have now and ahead of us. I think leaving the police and running the South Shore Inn was the best move we've made."

"I agree," John said. "There were good things about the conference. The trip, the break, gave me perspective. I'm glad I went. Best of all, we met. My life with you and Leah is everything I could ever wish for."

"Same here." Rebecca took John's hand. "I love it here, and I am so happy not to be in New York anymore, especially with the pandemic raging. And I think we'll be fine even though we have had very few guests. We do have a couple coming in tomorrow afternoon. They are staying for a week. I'm looking forward to meeting them. I've heard of the wife,

Fiona. Not a lot. But folks speak very highly of her. She's a social worker who specializes in helping kids who've been sexually abused, and she runs some sort of abuse prevention or awareness program in the schools. Apparently, she's had a couple of major challenges recently."

"Like what?" John asked.

"Well, I heard that she and her husband had a foster kid. They have three adopted children by the way, though they are not coming. Their foster kid was a victim of her biological mother's boyfriend. He went after other kids too, apparently always children of whoever he was dating. He was that sexual predator that was in the papers when they finally got him. I can't remember if that was last year or a couple of years ago."

"I remember. Wasn't one of my cases, but he'd talk kids into posing for him, usually naked or semi-naked, take photos, and then if they didn't give in to his sexual demands, he'd post the photos online. He was sent to jail for a long time. He was being kept in solitary for fear other inmates would do him in. Didn't help, he was killed in jail. Alexander somebody."

"That's the one. Anyway, this Fiona woman's foster kid ended up running away and overdosing on the streets of Toronto. And then the second tragedy about a year later. Her husband, who used to be a church minister, had a major breakdown or stroke, and stopped speaking. They were on a family vacation and no one seems to know what happened. They apparently went to a conference in Vancouver, and when they came back, he was a mess. He was in an institution for ages, and I think someone said he is still getting therapy."

"Maybe their week here without the kids is part of his therapy. We do have a reputation of being a soul restoring place. It worked for us," said John.

"And it sure worked for Calypso. She was the most anxious puppy I've ever heard of when we first got her. Someone was saying that after the first tragedy, Fiona and Ian's church sent them on a month-long retreat to Thailand. But of course, they can't go back there now, with the travel restrictions. I've always wanted to go to Asia."

"Well, once this pandemic is over, maybe we could go. We should talk to them about their trip, maybe get some ideas on places to go and things to do."

"Leah, Calypso, come back, it's time to go home."

All the incidents of child abuse in this novel are fictional. However, I am sorry to say that they are all too typical of horrific incidents of child abuse and child neglect that are widely documented. And, unfortunately, I have seen first-hand the devastating results that child neglect, abuse, and sexual abuse can have, sometimes destroying lives years after the child has left the harmful environment. Several case histories are included in my academic books, including *Children, Families and Violence* (2009) and *The Challenge of Children's Rights for Canada* (2018).

If you are looking for help for yourself or a child you know, there are many reputable agencies. A good place to start is with your local Child Protection Agency.

Katherine Covell is a developmental psychologist and children's rights advocate with a long history of academic books and articles. This is her first novel. She has been trying to write one since she was eight years old. She lives in Vancouver, British Columbia, Canada.